"So tell me—why are you after my money?"

Stallard Beauchamp's voice was tough, his eyes steely.

"I'm not," Farran exploded, his question making her want to get away from the hateful brute. But for her stepsister's sake, and for Uncle Henry's sake, she had to stay. "I have my own money," she went on defiantly, struggling to control her temper.

"Then perhaps, Farran," Stallard said mockingly, "you should tell me why you're here and what it is that you do want?"

"I want . . ." she began in a hurried rush, then stopped abruptly. Even unsaid, as she tried out the words in her head, they sounded blunt, money-grabbing and totally avaricious.

As he silently held her gaze, she knew it was crunch time. If there was anything she wanted—it was up to her to tell him now!

Jessica Steele first tried her hand at writing romance novels at her husband's encouragement two years after they were married. She fondly remembers the day her first novel was accepted for publication. ''Peter mopped me up, and neither of us cooked that night,'' she recalls. ''We went out to dinner.'' She and her husband live in a hundred-year-old cottage in Worcestershire, and they've traveled to many fascinating places—such as China, Japan, Mexico and Denmark—that make wonderful settings for her books.

Books by Jessica Steele

HARLEQUIN ROMANCE

HARLEQUIN PRESENTS

UNFRIENDLY PROPOSITION

Jessica Steele

Harlequin Books

TORONTO • NEW YORK • LONDON
AMSTERDAM • PARIS • SYDNEY • HAMBURG
STOCKHOLM • ATHENS • TOKYO • MILAN

Original hardcover edition published in 1989
by Mills & Boon Limited

ISBN 0-373-03095-9

Harlequin Romance first edition December 1990
Harlequin Romance second edition January 1991

CHAPTER ONE

HER first mistake, Farran Henderson painfully acknowledged, had been to fall in love with a married man to start with. Her second mistake, her second and *glaring* mistake, had been to imagine that Russell Ottley had, for a single moment, returned her love.

She glanced out of the window of the aircraft bringing her home from Hong Kong, where she had been working for the last ten months. By the look of it, she mused unhappily as the plane began its descent into Gatwick, January in England was as bleak and as gloomy as her spirits.

Her thoughts were soon far from England, however, and were back where they had been throughout the long flight—in Hong Kong. Oh, what a fool she had made of herself!

It was no wonder to her that she had more or less resigned on the spot without staying to work out the last two months of her contract. Apart from anything else, it was taking her all her time to live with the embarrassment of having more or less thrown herself at her boss, without having to live with the embarrassing memory of...

As if still unable to face the credulous fool she had made of herself, Farran broke off her thoughts. Crossly, though, she thought of how she *hadn't* thrown herself at Russell Ottley to begin with. To begin with, she had used all the will power at her command to prevent him from knowing how she felt about him.

She dwelt for a moment or two on how it had all begun. Love had been far from her mind when, after working for Yeo International for three years, she had spotted the vacancy being advertised in the staff magazine. She had applied immediately, but competition had been fierce for the secretarial position in the insurance branch of the Hong Kong office. Which had made it so much more gratifying when she had been advised that, out of all of them, she had been the one selected.

Hong Kong had been everything she had read about and more, and it just had to be one of the most exciting places in the world—those were her first impressions when she got there. Then she had met her new boss, Russell Ottley, and her impressions of Hong Kong had soon faded into the background.

It had not taken her long to discover that Russell was married, and that he also had a couple of children. The one piece of information, even without the other, was enough to have Farran mentally tagging him with a 'Do not touch' label. But in no time she was beginning to get the idea, from a word he said here and there, that Russell was not happily married, and after three months of working for him, with Russell hinting that his wife was talking of leaving him, the writing on the 'Do not touch' label had started to become blurred.

She had been working for him for six months, however, when, having up till then steadfastly refused to confront what she felt for him, Farran finally faced up to the fact that she loved him.

Three months after that she was beginning to see that Russell might feel the same way about her—and she went through agonies about that. Valiantly, though, she urged him to try, and to keep on trying, to save his marriage.

Being only human, however, and aware by then from things he had let fall that his marriage was as good as dead, she could not help but feel something inside whenever in the next month he looked at her in that special way, or called her 'light of my life'. Nor could she fail to be moved when occasionally he would slip up and, tenderly, call her 'darling'.

Things had nearly come to a peak a few days before when, having an hour or so earlier told her that his wife seemed to be packing everything but the kitchen sink—and thereby giving Farran the impression that he and his wife were separating—he'd left his desk and come over to hers. He was about to pass when, as she looked at him, he suddenly caught hold of her. 'Don't you know what being near you does to me?' he had asked in a tortured kind of voice.

But just then she had not been ready—she hadn't at that point got things worked out in her head—and hurriedly she had pulled away from him. 'It's... I...' she had faltered, and had speedily made for the cloakroom.

It was in the cloakroom that Farran realised that things had gone too far now for her to try and pretend that they meant nothing to each other. It was there, though, that she suddenly started to think of what, because of her family background of broken marriages, she had resolutely avoided thinking of so far—that there might be a chance for her and Russell.

Though, the way she saw it, if his wife was leaving him, and his marriage was over, then full consideration must be given to his children, of that she was certain. Farran supposed it was fair to say that her own childhood had not been one of the best. Which again was probably why she had fought against the love she had for Russell which might in some way harm his children.

She relived the confusion of her parents separating and then divorcing. Life had become more settled when her mother had subsequently married Henry Preston. Dear, vague, lovable Uncle Henry! He had been married before, too, and had a daughter five years older than

Farran. But his second marriage had worked out no better than his first. Worse, in fact, for when her mother, declaring him 'utterly impossible', had walked out and started divorce proceedings, she had left behind her thirteen-year-old daughter for him to look after, and Farran had known yet more confusion.

She therefore formed the view that if matters were handled properly there was no need for Russell's children to know any of that same confusion.

She returned to her desk and, because she felt she had rebuffed him, gave Russell a warm smile. Having at last got everything sorted out in her head, she was now eager to tell him how she felt about him, and eager to hear him state his love for her. But, in discovering that, since his marriage was finished, yes, she could be sufficiently modern to accept the role of the second Mrs Ottley, she also discovered that she was still old-fashioned enough to believe that the first move had to come from him.

Two days were to pass, however, before Farran, in an agony of waiting, suddenly realised that Russell was about to declare himself.

It was Thursday morning and she looked up to find he was not attending to the matters in front of him, but was staring directly at her.

Remembering the rebuff she had served him two days before, she had no intention of dealing him another, when the whole weekend would pass, or even longer, before he declared himself.

'Something—er—bothering you?' she had gently, smilingly invited.

'You could say that,' he replied and, encouraged by her smile, he was suddenly over by her desk.

Farran was on her feet when, at the responsive look in her eyes, he grabbed her in a passionate embrace. For a few moments then, as his mouth greedily devoured hers, time stood still.

'Russell!' she sighed as she came up for air.

'Now you know what's bothering me,' he told her softly, and there was a seductive note in his voice that thrilled her.

'Yes,' she replied, and was so thrilled by this intimation that he loved her that she fairly launched herself at him.

Russell was the first one to speak when their next kiss ended, and there was a feverish look on his face. 'Whew, Farran!' he exclaimed. 'I thought you might be hot stuff, but I'm going to have my work cut out if this is just a sample!'

Thrilled by what she took to be his confirmation that he did indeed love her and that he was declaring that theirs was to be a permanent relationship, Farran again eagerly met him more than half-way. Again they kissed, her response more enthusiastic than ever.

Suddenly, though, through the passion of the moment, memories of her bewildered childhood were nudging her conscience, and she eased herself out from his tight embrace.

'We—have to talk,' she told him quietly.

'If you're willing,' Russell came back promptly, 'and I can see that you are, we could spend the weekend together.'

At first she was not sure what she felt about that. 'Where?' she asked, her serious large brown eyes fixed on his face.

'Where else but at my flat?' he replied with a smile.

'Oh, Russell!' she cried softly, knowing then that his wife had returned to England and his marriage must have ended.

'Will you?' he asked.

'Spend the weekend with you in your flat?' she queried.

'It seems as good a place as any,' he responded, and tacked on smilingly, 'We can—er—talk all you like then.'

'The children's welfare has to be of prime importance,' Farran told him seriously, not knowing as yet if his wife had taken them back to England with her or, like her own mother, had left her offspring with her husband.

Only as she saw Russell's look of surprise at her statement, however, did it dawn on her that he had maybe not thought she would be so understanding of his, or their, responsibility to his children. She was a little startled just the same when he replied, 'I can't see that their welfare has got anything to do with you and me, sweetness.'

From that Farran could only gather that his wife must have taken the children back to England with her and that he must be a little touchy on the subject. But, with his children's welfare uppermost in her mind, 'They'll have everything to do with us when they come out from England to pay us a visit,' she told him gently.

Russell, though, did not merely startle her, but shattered her rosy dreams completely, destroying any idea she had that his wife had taken the children to England— or that she had in fact left Hong Kong herself. 'Pay us a visit?' he echoed. And as a penny seemed to drop, 'Strewth, Farran,' he exclaimed, 'I only meant you should come to my place for the weekend—not that you should move in! How could you, anyway, when the wife and kids will be back from their trip to Lantau Island on Monday? I don't think . . .'

What he thought, Farran did not stay around to hear. Mortified at the utter fool she had just made of herself, she raced away and hid herself and her humiliation from him and the outside world by locking herself in one of the cubicles in the cloakroom.

She was still mortified and not thinking very clearly when, working on auto-pilot, she returned to her office and, observing that Russell was for the moment absent, typed out her resignation. She left the building and on reaching the sanctuary of her small flat made her first task that of ringing the airport.

The first available flight was that evening, which left her little time in which to pack her belongings and settle any outstanding accounts and business matters in Hong Kong. By the skin of her teeth Farran made that flight.

The thud of tyres on tarmac as the plane touched down brought her out of her reverie. An hour later she was on her way to the small town of Banford, the only home she knew, and which lay in the county of Buckinghamshire.

Uncle Henry, her stepfather, would be surprised to see her, she mused at one point in her journey. Or, on the other hand, maybe he wouldn't. Henry Preston was an inventor of gadgets which had no practical use, or which, if useful, took more time to use than the job could otherwise be performed in. Depending on the degree of absorption which he was giving his present invention— and he always had at least one invention on the go—he might well have absently forgotten that he hadn't seen her for ten months.

Having not been to bed in over twenty-four hours, Farran felt not only emotionally drained but bone-weary when somewhere around mid-morning she struggled with her luggage up the garden path of her stepfather's home. Her dear stepfather was not the first person she saw, however, but, cheerfully polishing the brass door knob, Mrs Fenner, their cheerful 'heart-of-gold' housekeeper, who had been with them for a good number of years.

'Well, I never!' she beamed in total surprise when she saw Farran. And, coming to help her with her luggage, she exclaimed, 'Mr Preston never said anything about you being expected!' Then, with the ease of one who was well thought of in the household, she grinned, showing off her fine set of dentures. 'But then he's so involved with his latest barm-pot idea, I'm sure he doesn't know whether he's on this earth or fuller's!'

'I didn't let Uncle Henry know I was coming,' Farran informed her as she shook hands with her, suddenly glad to be home where nothing, and certainly not Mrs Fenner and her bright sense of humour, had changed. 'Is he in his workshop?' she asked.

'Where else?' Mrs Fenner replied, and when Farran headed in that direction she called after her. 'I'll put the coffee pot on.'

Farran entered her stepfather's workshop and, re-alising that he had not heard her, stood for a moment observing his dear bent head. He was in his fifty-ninth year, and although he had never had a paid job in his life he was always busy at something. At one time the Prestons had been wealthy, but that was no longer the case. As she looked at the dear man, his brow knitted as he puzzled over some problem, a wave of affection for him washed over her, and suddenly it did not seem to her that her mother had done such a dreadful thing in leaving her in this home. Georgia, Henry Preston's daughter, had been eighteen then, and although she was involved with pursuits of her own Farran had always got on well with her.

Farran reasoned then that her mother must have talked it over with Henry before leaving, and that they must have mutually agreed that it was better at this stage in her development to stay put, rather than go through the upheaval of changing schools as well as everything else.

Neither father nor daughter had ever made her feel unwelcome in their home, though, and all at once Farran felt overwhelmingly grateful that never once had either Henry Preston or Georgia thrown back at her how they had given her a home when her mother had walked out. Consequently, her voice was slightly choky as she called softly, 'Uncle Henry!'

'Where have you sprung from?' Henry Preston queried, swinging round in astonishment. 'It's not twelve months since you went away, is it?' he asked, his face starting to beam as he left his work-bench and, despite his grubby overall, once white and in defiance of all efforts white no longer, gave her a huge hug and a kiss.

Farran was mildly surprised that he had remembered her contract had been for a twelve-month period, and shook her head as she replied, 'Not quite.' She was mystified by his next question, though.

'They didn't ring you too, did they?' he asked.

In honour of the occasion of her homecoming, Henry Preston shed his overall, left his workshop and went with his stepdaughter to the sitting-room, where a minute or so later Mrs Fenner brought them a tray of coffee.

It was over a cup of coffee that Farran was able to make some sense of her stepfather's question about someone ringing her too. The clarification of which succeeded in taking her mind off her feelings over the events in her personal life, only to make her feel sad over another event. For it transpired that her stepfather had been telephoned by a Mrs King about an hour ago and had been informed that his only other blood relative— apart from his daughter—had passed away the previous day.

'Aunt Hetty's dead?' Farran questioned in quiet regret, having made the elderly lady's acquaintance some ten years earlier—the 'Aunt' title, though, being the same courtesy title as the 'Uncle' she had been instructed to call Henry Preston.

'I'm afraid so. Mrs King rang to tell me that the funeral is next Tuesday.' Some minutes followed while they spoke respectfully of Miss Hetty Newbold, the lady of eighty-one years whom Farran had visited often and in whose home she and Georgia had over the years stayed overnight several times. Then Henry was telling her, 'Georgia had left for work when Mrs King phoned, so I rang and told her, and she said that since it seems that this Mrs King must have been one of Aunt Hetty's bridge cronies and appears to have quite capably seen to all the arrangements, there seems little point in her taking time off to go down to Dorset before next Tuesday. She's up to her ears in it at the salon, apparently.'

'That's good—that her business is so busy, I mean,' Farran qualified, shaking off sad thoughts of Aunt Hetty to feel enormously proud of her stepsister and the success which talent and hard work had earned her since she had established Banford's first high street beauty salon three years before.

Some seconds ticked by as she dwelt on how Georgia had ambitions to own a chain of beauty salons, then weariness began to prod at her just as her stepfather was querying, 'Are you going into town to see Georgia?'

Farran managed to dredge up a smile. Quite obviously Uncle Henry had something of the utmost importance to him going on in his workshop—twenty minutes away from it and he was getting withdrawal symptoms! 'Actually,' she replied, 'I was thinking more of going to bed.'

Instantly he was all apologies. 'How thoughtless of me!' he exclaimed. 'Of course, to get here at this time of day, you must have flown through the night. We'll get Mrs Fenner to make your room ready and...' He broke off as Mrs Fenner came in to see if they had finished with the coffee tray.

'Farran's room has been kept aired and ready for her since she went away,' their salt-of-the-earth housekeeper sniffed politely, 'and I've just this minute finished making up her bed for her,' and turning to Farran, 'I thought you looked as though a few hours' kip might do you some good,' she commented.

As weary as she felt, however, it took Farran some while to get any rest. No sooner was she on her own again than thoughts of Mrs Fenner, Uncle Henry, Georgia and even Aunty Hetty vanished from her mind. Oh, how *could* she have been so stupid! She was twenty-three years old, for goodness' sake! How could she have been so—so naïve?

Pulling the bedcovers up over her head, she faced the unpalatable truth that, all the while she had been thinking in rosy wholesome pictures of love, love had never been in Russell's mind. He had never loved her, that much was abundantly plain. All he had wanted, she was painfully forced to accept, was a sordid adulterous affair—in the home he shared with his wife and family, too!

The ugly truth had to be faced, just as Farran honestly faced the fact that she had been in error too. She had known, had she not, that he was married? Although if she wanted excuses for her own behaviour then she had truly believed that his marriage had gone beyond the saving stage before she had stopped fighting and had allowed herself to think in terms of her future lying with him.

To her surprise, when she did eventually get to sleep, she slept soundly—though since she had quite a lot of sleep to catch up on, perhaps it was not so surprising. Some sound in her room awakened her, however, and she opened her eyes, to wonder at first where she was, and then to realise exactly where. Before she could again open up what was a new and raw wound, though, her tall, slim stepsister suddenly stepped into her line of vision.

'So you came personally to see why I never answered one of your letters, huh?' queried Georgia, by way of greeting and apology for never putting pen to paper.

'You never did like paperwork,' Farran smiled, having nothing to forgive and moving to sit up in bed to accept the cup of tea her stepsister had brought up for her.

'It gives me nightmares,' the blonde Georgia agreed, as she studied Farran's fine features and shoulder-length, shiny dark brown hair. 'But since it's an essential part of running any business I'm stuck with it.' She paused, then studied the pale look to her younger stepsister's perfect complexion. 'What went wrong?' she queried quietly.

'I...' Farran began, then added, 'I've thrown up my job,' and got as far as, 'I—he...' when her voice faded.

'A man, huh?' Georgia calculated, twenty-eight and more worldly-wise than Farran. She did not press her, however, but suggested, 'You can tell me about it when you feel like it, but meantime, Mrs Fenner has gone to town on dinner tonight, so...'

'I'll get up straight away,' Farran said quickly. Ten minutes later, as the smell of home cooking assailed her nostrils, she realised that she was starving.

She was again grateful to Georgia for her tact when at dinner that evening, Henry Preston, as if believing he had been lax, started questioning Farran about Hong Kong. For it was Georgia who interrupted to change the subject. The matter under discussion from then on was Miss Hetty Newbold's demise.

'Poor old dear!' murmured Georgia. The family blood-link with the elderly lady was somewhat obscure. 'I should have made time to go and see her, or at least found the time to write to her,' she regretted, then looked suddenly startled, as if something had only then dawned on her. 'I can't remember the last time I made the trip to High Monkton.'

'Hasn't anybody been to see her since I left?' Farran exclaimed, startled herself at the thought. Prior to going to Hong Kong, and initially at their behest, she had used her Saturdays or Sundays to visit the village of High Monkton on behalf of both Georgia and her father. Aunt Hetty had always been so pleased to see her and to hear the family news that Farran, having grown fond of her, had thereafter occasionally visited her without their bidding.

'You know how it is,' Henry Preston excused. 'Georgia and I are always so tied up, and anyway, when I did pick up the phone to see how she was getting on—some months back—all I got for my trouble was some sarcastic reference like, had I given up driving the car now that I was nearing sixty?'

'She could have a bit of a sharp tongue sometimes,' Farran had to admit. 'But she loved you both dearly, and...'

'Which is why,' Georgia cut in, 'the old love has left Dad and me her fortune.'

'It's only natural that she should,' Farran stated, knowing, to use Georgia's phrase, that Aunt Hetty 'wasn't short of a bob or two'. She was startled, however, at Georgia's dry reply.

'I'm in dead trouble if she hasn't,' she announced, but was quite relaxed as she added, 'Though, since she showed me a copy of her will the last time I was there, I shouldn't think I've got anything to worry about.'

'You've—got money troubles?' asked Farran.

'Who hasn't?' Georgia replied.

'But I thought your business was doing so well!'

'It is,' Georgia confirmed, 'but not well enough to finance the purchase of the greengrocer's shop next door which has just come up for sale.'

'You want to open a greengrocer's?' her father came out of his contemplation of the tablecloth to enquire, and Georgia rolled her eyes to the ceiling.

'No, dear, I don't want to open a greengrocer's,' she replied, but excitement was in her eyes as she added, 'Ever since your phone call to the salon this morning I've been chasing here, there and everywhere. First there was the Town Planning Department to contact to see how they felt about a change of usage. But, since Banford already has more greengrocers than it needs, there was no problem there.'

'Ah, you're thinking of changing the greengrocer's into another beauty parlour,' her father cottoned on.

'Got it in one,' Georgia told him, and was addressing both her father and Farran when she told them, 'Though I intend to enlarge the one I've got rather than have two salons. Which,' she smiled, 'is why I've had to see builders, estate agents, solicitors and bankers too today.'

Farran was not very sure how she felt about what she was hearing. For it seemed to her that Aunt Hetty had barely drawn her last breath than, on the strength of the half-share of a fortune she would inherit, Georgia had set about spending it.

'Things—er—seem to be moving fast,' she commented.

'You can't let the grass grow in business,' Georgia asserted, and revealed, 'With the bank's help, I've already secured the property.'

The weekend passed quietly, Saturday being the busiest day of the week for Georgia, while Farran stayed home and sorted out her unpacking and her wardrobe. Discussion at dinner that night centred again on Aunt Hetty's fortune, with this time Henry Preston realising that the purchase of a new lathe he sorely desired might well now be within his sights.

On Sunday Farran helped Georgia with her paper-work and, with all figures entered into ledgers by lunchtime, it was agreed over lunch that the three of them would travel down to High Monkton in Georgia's car for Aunt Hetty's funeral on Tuesday.

On Monday Farran breakfasted with Georgia, who then, with the light of excitement in her eyes, went off to her place of business. Farran went upstairs to look for something suitable to wear to the funeral and to re-alise that she would soon have to do something about getting a job. She was unable just then to find any en-thusiasm for anything, however.

Georgia was later coming in that night than she had intimated that morning. Henry Preston had had his dinner and had returned to his workshop when Georgia finally came home and complained to Farran how she'd had not one but two stylists go off sick, and how she'd been rushed off her feet finding cover for them. 'Then the builder who said he'd be there at five didn't turn up, so I had to phone him and he said he was on his way, but he didn't arrive until gone six.'

'You're having some building done?'

'Alterations,' Georgia corrected. 'I borrowed the keys of the shop next door to show the builder round, but only to find that the wretched man was more concerned with telling me what I couldn't have done—something to do with main beams and building regulations—than with what I wanted. The result being that, after a phone call to an architect, the three of us are meeting at eleven in the morning for an on-site discussion. How I'm going to find the time, since I doubt that Linda and Christy will be in again before Thursday, I don't know, but...'

'I hate to give you more pressure,' Farran cut in quietly, 'but you *have* remembered that Aunt Hetty is being buried at midday tomorrow?'

'Oh, lord!' Georgia exclaimed, aghast. 'I'd for-gotten...' She thought swiftly for some moments. 'It's no good,' she came to a prompt conclusion, 'I just can't go. You and Dad will have to go without me.'

'There's—no way you could manage to attend?' Farran asked tentatively. To her mind, with Georgia being a blood relation of Aunt Hetty, no matter how obscure that relationship, it was more important that she attend than herself.

But Georgia was shaking her head. 'How?' she asked.

Farran saw her briefly the next morning at breakfast where, in an effort to get a head start, she was leaving for work early.

'Hope you have an easier day today,' Farran bade her as her stepsister made for the door.

'Pigs might fly!' quipped Georgia, and was almost through the door when she suddenly halted and then turned back. 'I've mentioned it to Dad, but he'll probably forget,' she said quickly. 'But, since you'll be going to Selborne before and after the funeral,' she hurried on, Selborne being the name of Aunt Hetty's house, 'would you pick up the will for me?'

'You don't think the Mrs King who's arranged every-thing won't have passed the will over to Aunt Hetty's solicitor?' asked Farran, after taking a second or two to hop on to her stepsister's wavelength.

'I shouldn't think so for a minute,' Georgia replied. 'Only the closest of family would know that the old dear kept her private papers in a biscuit tin at the back of that antiquated wardrobe in her dressing-room.'

Feeling a special warmth for her stepsister for the way she had included her in that phrase 'the closest of family', since Aunt Hetty had several times shown her where the biscuit tin reposed, Farran smiled her agreement to bringing the will back to her. Georgia stayed long enough to comment that, in order to speed things up, rather than forward the will to Aunt Hetty's solicitors, she would take it to her own solicitors on Wednesday. Then she left for work.

Thinking not to disturb her stepfather too early, Farran left it until there were about forty minutes to spare before they set out for the village of High Monkton before she went to tell him it was time for him to get ready.

As she neared his workshop door, however, she began to smell fumes of some kind. The smell grew stronger, and once inside the workshop—where fortunately the windows were wide open—she saw that it would take more than an hour and forty minutes to scrub her step-father clean.

'I've had a little accident with some sump oil,' he looked up to impart. To Farran's mind it looked as though he had not only attempted to flood the floor with it but, with his face and hair seeming to be begrimed with it, had taken a shower in it. 'It's only just happened, but I'd better clear the mess up first,' he told her.

Farran looked at him, looked at the floor, which appeared to be in need of vast quantities of detergent, and came to a decision. 'Can I borrow your car?' she asked him.

'Would you?' he caught on to ask happily.

Farran drove alone to High Monkton with depression descending every mile of the way. Her life suddenly appeared to be without direction.

A traffic jam en route caused her to review her plans. She was almost at High Monkton when she decided that there was little point in first visiting Selborne when barely a minute later she would have to leave the house to go to the church. In disconsolate mood, she made for High Monkton church.

Her sadness deepened when the pall-bearers brought in Miss Newbold's coffin. She offered up a prayer for her, but as the service began her thoughts somehow strayed. By the time the service was over, Farran was feeling more dejected than she had ever felt in her life.

She left the church trying desperately to push thoughts of Russell Ottley from her mind. He had no place here where she was paying her last respects to Aunt Hetty.

Swallowing hard, she was in the throes of trying to get a grip on herself when, all of a sudden, she had a feeling that someone was watching her. Abruptly she looked to her left, and immediately almost looked away again.

She did not look away, however, but, although she had not been aware if there had been ten people present at the service or a hundred, she was suddenly very much aware of the tall man who stood looking at her. Not merely looking either, but staring icily at her! Not quite believing it, for she was more used to men looking at her with a little admiration in their eyes, Farran looked again, but in that man's cold stare she could see no admiration. Indeed, far from admiration, all she could see in this man's look was steely-eyed contempt!

Slightly staggered that any man could look at her so contemptuously, or could be so contemptuous of her, Farran checked to see if she could have misread his look. She had not, she saw, for they stood with about ten feet separating them and she was close enough for her to note also his straight, arrogant nose and his firm, no-nonsense chin.

She decided, as he continued to look down his nose at her, that it was about time she gave him the benefit of her own uppity look. Before she could do so, though, the most disagreeable-looking elderly lady, wearing a re-markable large black hat complete with ostrich feather, who was holding on to his arm, said something to attract his attention.

Tilting her chin a fraction higher, Farran turned away and went to her car. Arrogant swine! she dubbed the tall stranger. Who the dickens did he think he was, to look at her in that fashion?

She didn't care a button anyway, she told herself as she unlocked the car. Unless he was going back to the house—and there was something about him that suggested he was too busy for that—she wasn't going to see him again.

Somehow it never occurred to her that, from feeling deeply depressed and unable to get Russell Ottley out of her mind, she was now feeling angry, and had not given thought to Russell Ottley for a good few minutes.

CHAPTER TWO

To Farran's annoyance she did see the man again. She owned to feeling somewhat reluctant to go to Selborne and would much have preferred to have motored back to Banford. However, Georgia was anxious to present Aunt Hetty's will to the solicitors tomorrow, so there was nothing for it but to point the car in the direction of Aunt Hetty's house.

When Farran walked into Miss Newbold's home she did not recognise anyone there. There were fewer than a dozen people assembled when she entered the sitting-room, mostly, apart from *him*, seeming to be elderly matrons. Farran spotted *him* straight away, though she pretended that she hadn't. He was standing near the elderly and disagreeable-looking woman with the hat whom she had seen earlier, who was seated and was disagreeably instructing a fiftyish-year-old, intense-looking woman to go and do something or other.

When the intense-looking woman scurried away and the tall man bent to address some remark to the elderly lady, Farran had a chance to cast more than a passing glance in their direction. His straight nose and firm chin were as she remembered them, she saw, observing that there was an outdoor look to him, probably because his fair hair was sun-streaked.

At a guess she thought he would be somewhere in his mid-thirties—could he be the sour-looking woman's son? If she was a contemporary of Aunt Hetty, though, who had been eighty-one, it seemed possible that he was more likely to be grandson than son. But since he had the

24

same sour look to him—when he had looked at her in the churchyard, anyway—then he just had to be related.

When it seemed, however, that he was just about to look her way, Farran swiftly turned her glance away from him. Just at that moment a wiry-looking woman carrying a tray came and stood in front of her.

'Would you like a cup of tea?' the woman asked.

'Not just now, thank you,' Farran declined politely, but suddenly she realised that, since she was her family's representative, maybe she ought to set about finding Mrs King to thank her for making all the arrangements. 'Are you Mrs King?' she asked the woman quietly before she moved on.

'I'm Mrs Allsopp,' the woman introduced herself. 'I cleaned for Miss Newbold on Mondays and Thursdays.' She then seemed to realise from Farran's quiet tone that she did not want attention drawn to her enquiry, and told her in a quieter voice, 'I can't say I know a Mrs King, but I can ask around for you if you like?'

'No, that's all right,' Farran assured her, wondering in passing, since this was Tuesday, who if not Mrs King had arranged for Mrs Allsopp to come to Selborne to dispense tea today.

Mrs Allsopp went on her way as Farran recalled that she had heard Aunt Hetty mention the cleaning woman's name, though since her visits to Selborne had only ever been at the weekend, she had never met her.

Realising that going upstairs and rummaging around among Aunt Hetty's personal belongings was a chore she would rather not have, Farran faced the fact that she could not return to Banford without the will. But even though she personally felt there was something 'not quite nice' about what she had to do, she made herself think only of the fact that, by virtue of her connections with Georgia and her father, she had more right in the house, and in any room in the house, than anyone there.

Determining to find Mrs King later to thank her for all she had done, Farran decided to go and get the will, the sooner to have it all over with.

Even as she silently reiterated that she had more right there than anyone, though, she nevertheless hoped that if anyone saw her leave the sitting-room and make for the stairs, they would assume she was making for the upstairs bathroom.

Never having thought for a moment that she would feel so awkward when it came to carrying out her step-sister's straightforward request, Farran went into Miss Newbold's bedroom and headed for the adjoining dressing-room. Swiftly, she went over to the wardrobe in the dressing-room and, stooping down, quickly extracted the biscuit tin—which was just where it had always been.

She was still stooped down and ready to transfer the will to her handbag when she pulled open the lid of the tin and, to her astonishment, discovered that the tin was empty!

That was not all. She was still suffering shock when, to astonish her further—not to say shatter her completely—she suddenly realised that she was not alone. Someone had followed her.

'Is this what you're looking for?' an educated and arrogant male voice addressed her back.

Uncertain that she had not jumped a foot, Farran instinctively knew, without question, to whom the voice belonged. Shaken though she was, however, she straightened slowly and unhurriedly turned around. As she had known, it *was* the tall, fair, sun-streaked-haired stranger. In his hand he held a folded sheet of parchment.

'If that happens to be the will of Miss Hetty Newbold,' Farran began, striving hard for a cool note, 'then I believe that I have more right to it than you.' So saying, she held out a hand to take it from him.

He made no attempt to give it to her, however, but instead drawled, 'I think not.'

'What do you mean?' she snapped, some of her cool manner too soon departing. 'I've more rights than...'

'You have no rights,' he sliced in shortly. 'Under Miss Newbold's previous will you might have done very nicely, but...'

'She changed her will?' Farran butted in, aghast at the very idea. Georgia was banking on...

'I'm afraid so,' the tall stranger broke in, and looked more pleased to be able to confirm that than sorry to have to be the one to break the news, Farran thought. 'In her new will—her *last* will,' he stressed, 'it seems that you have been cut out. You, it appears,' he smiled silkily, 'inherit not so much as a brass farthing.'

'I...' Farran gasped, suddenly hating this arrogant, false-smiled conveyor of bad news, 'I—don't believe you,' she got herself together to challenge on Georgia's behalf. 'I know for a fact,' she gathered up a head of steam, 'that Miss Newbold willed her estate to...'

'To one,' the man chipped in again, 'Stallard Beauchamp.' And while Farran was momentarily stunned into silence, looking every bit as though he was starting to quite enjoy telling her what he had, he mockingly passed the piece of parchment over to her.

Feeling suddenly stifled in the small dressing-room, Farran took the will from him and went past him into the bedroom. Then, hoping against hope that he was telling lies, she opened up the parchment and quickly began to read.

A few minutes later, totally unable to believe that it was just as he had said, and that everything Miss Newbold had possessed had been left to some man whom she, and she was sure Georgia too, had never heard of, Farran read through the will again, more slowly this time. By the time she had read it through a second time, though, and with the name Stallard Beauchamp appearing everywhere—Georgia's name and that of Henry Preston not appearing once—she was so winded that she had wit left only to check the date of the legal document. It was dated less than a month ago.

What this would mean to Georgia's plans was still sinking in when Farran looked up to see that the tall man was surveying her with a most annoying sardonic expression. His expression riled her, and she demanded sharply, 'Who *is* this Stallard Beauchamp?'

'Huh!' the man scorned, that contemptuous look back on his face. 'Your grief-stricken act in the churchyard didn't last very long, did it!' and as realisation hit Farran that the reason for his look of contempt in the churchyard was that he thought she had been acting grief-stricken—when in actual fact her thoughts had been more on her non-affair with Russell than with poor Aunt Hetty—he drawled, 'Allow me to introduce myself.'

Farran saw then that, since he had been the one in possession of the will, had she not felt so stunned, she would have worked out who he was for herself. But, feeling that she needed some time to pull herself together, she handed him back the will and checked, 'You're Stallard Beauchamp?'

'The same,' he nodded, and questioned sarcastically, 'Which grieving mourner are you—Georgia Preston or Farran Henderson?'

Farran was again shaken. How did this objectionable man know her name? 'I'm Farran Henderson,' she told him shortly. 'How is it you've heard of me, when I've never heard of you?'

He was completely unconcerned by her demanding manner. 'The names Georgia Preston, Henry Preston and Farran Henderson appear in Miss Newbold's previous will,' he told her offhandedly.

'I—see,' Farran said haltingly, seeing very little except that Georgia could say goodbye to any chance of buying the greengrocer's, and that, by the look of it, Aunt Hetty must have added a codicil to her previous will, leaving her some small legacy too.

Farran, however, was hard put to it not to show her amazement when it transpired that, in her previous will, Miss Newbold had left her more than some small legacy when Stallard Beauchamp mocked loftily, 'The spoils, Miss Henderson, were to be divided equally among the three of you. Such a pity,' he taunted, 'that the personal effects tin which Mrs Allsopp handed over to me also contained this will.' Arrogantly he waved the will in Farran's general direction. 'This will,' he smiled insincerely, 'revokes all others. Which means,' he enlightened her, just in case she had not worked it out for herself, 'that neither you nor your step-relatives inherit a thing.'

Farran was by then of the opinion that Stallard Beauchamp just had to be about the most hateful human being she had ever come across. All too obviously he thought her only reason for being there that day was to pick up Miss Newbold's will. Dearly did she want to tell him that she had come to High Monkton purely out of respect for the elderly lady. But, even as she opened her mouth to tell him just that, she knew it was not true. She would have come for Miss Newbold's funeral, of course she would, but she had come to the house, had climbed the staircase, on Georgia's errand.

Having opened her mouth to say something, however, she recalled that he knew of her step-relationship with Georgia and her father. But what about him? 'Who are you?' she asked abruptly, and when he looked down his arrogant nose as though to say, what the devil has that got to do with you, 'You're not related to Miss Newbold!'

she told him, a shade arrogantly herself. 'I know that for a fact.'

'I've no blood connection,' he agreed, his eyes narrowing at her haughty manner. 'I didn't feel, however, that I had to be related, or connected by a family relationship, to pay an elderly lady everyday courtesies in passing.'

'You've made a point of visiting her?'

'I've been to this house many times in this last year,' he replied, and, his voice taking on a tough note, 'Where have you and your step-relatives been this last twelve months?' he demanded to know.

Heartily Farran wished she could have told him that either her stepsister or stepfather had been to visit Aunt Hetty in the last year. But, since she was unable to do that, all she could do was to draw his attention from them, and speak for herself. 'I've been working in Hong Kong,' she told him sharply, and, it appeared, said totally the wrong thing when she added, 'I only came back last Friday.'

'Ye gods, you didn't waste any time!' Stallard Beauchamp hurled at her aggressively.

'What do you mean by that?' snapped Farran, angry sparks flashing from her normally tranquil brown eyes.

'What would I mean,' he charged toughly, 'other than that with Miss Newbold dying on Thursday, you must have caught the first treasure trail plane home that you could!'

'I didn't know she was dead until I arrived!' Farran protested furiously, feeling suddenly that it would give her a great deal of pleasure to be able to physically set about this awful man.

'Of course you didn't!' he scorned, clearly not believing a word of her protest. 'And of course it was only by accident that you wandered in here, and then wandered into Miss Newbold's dressing-room. What more natural than, having realised you'd made a mistake, you should then proceed to rifle through something that doesn't belong to you in order to get your greedy little hands on the document which you believed would entitle you to a third share of her estate!'

Farran gave him a spearing look and wished he didn't seem the sort who would exact full retribution if she aimed a kick at one of his shins. She had no defence, though, against his charge that she had entered Miss Newbold's dressing-room to rifle through something which did not belong to her. She thanked him not, however, for making her feel small—even if any rifling that had gone on had been for Georgia, and not for herself. But, having been made to feel small, she saw that her only defence lay in attack.

With what dignity she could muster she started to march past him towards the door. 'You're welcome to your inheritance,' she told him waspishly as she went. 'You've quite obviously worked hard over the last twelve months to get it!'

Any hopes she might have nursed of sailing out of the room having had the last word, however, were doomed, she was soon to realise. For plainly Stallard Beauchamp was a man who always had the honour when it came to last words.

'Being the type of woman you are,' he sneered before she could get the door open, 'I shouldn't have believed you'd think anything else.'

Farran was almost back in Banford before she had cooled down. In her view Stallard Beauchamp was one of the nastiest pieces of work she had ever come across! But, after she had silently called him every unpleasant name she could bring to mind, it suddenly dawned on her that instead of spending her time on thoughts of him, what she should be using her energies on was in trying to find the kindest way to tell Georgia what she had to be told.

As she let herself into the house, the first person Farran saw was Henry Preston, and only then did it occur to her that she had forgotten how much the inheritance would mean to him too! He had set his heart on a new lathe, and since nobody had given a thought to the notion that Miss Newbold might have recently changed her will, not once but twice, Farran realised that he could have very well already ordered his new lathe.

'Did everything go off all right?' he enquired, pausing to greet her on his way to his workshop.

'The funeral went off all right,' Farran told him, 'but...'

Her 'but' collided with his 'Good, good,' and not hearing that she was about to qualify her remark, he went on his way.

Perhaps, a cowardly voice tugged at her skirt, it would be better to tell him when Georgia was there. Perhaps then father and daughter could console one another over their lost fortune.

As it turned out, there was no consoling Georgia when she came in. She was unable to wait until they were seated round the dinner table, and no sooner was she inside the house than she came straight to the sitting-room where Farran was. 'Did you get it?' was her first question, bypassing any enquiry as to how the funeral had gone.

'I think you'd better sit down,' Farran replied, and as quickly as she could she relayed everything that had happened since she had had near heart failure on un-expectedly hearing Stallard Beauchamp's voice arro-gantly enquiring. 'Is this what you're looking for?'

'I don't believe it!' gasped Georgia, her face paling to make the blended-in rouge on her cheeks stand out markedly in contrast. She then insisted that Farran repeat everything again.

At the end of the second telling Farran's feelings were all the more on her stepsister's side, for Georgia was not at all put out of countenance to hear that the will had been changed the first time to include her in third portion of the estate. Georgia was very much put out, though, that some stranger should walk in and inherit the whole of Miss Newbold's estate.

Distraught as she was by what this would mean to her ideas for her business, Georgia shed a few angry tears as she declared, 'We have to have that inheritance. Aside from being fully extended at the bank, I've told too many clients, as well as friends, about my plans to back out now. I'll be the laughing stock of Banford if I don't go ahead!' she cried.

Farran spent most of the next day feeling very upset on her stepsister's behalf. At the same time, though, she could not help but love and admire the stoical way in which Henry Preston had handled his disappointment. For although, 'Oh, no!' was his first reaction on realising that he could say goodbye to any hope of a new lathe now, he was soon setting his mind to other matters—namely the invention which he was presently working on.

When Farran was not thinking of her stepsister or her stepfather that day, however, she would find herself thinking in turn of Russell Ottley, and then that other reptile of the species whose acquaintance she had had the misfortune to make yesterday. When thinking of Stallard Beauchamp only succeeded in making her angry, she pushed him out of her head by giving some thought to her unemployed state. As yet, the enthusiasm she needed to go and find herself a job evaded her.

As the time approached when Georgia was due home, Farran began to hope that her stepsister had started to come to terms with her disappointment over Aunt Hetty's will. And indeed, it seemed that her hopes had been fulfilled when, late again, Georgia came in that evening.

Farran was in the kitchen giving Mrs Fenner a hand when Georgia arrived home, however, and did not see her stepsister to speak to until she came to the dinner table. At once, and with some relief, Farran saw that she seemed more contented with her lot than she had last night.

Feeling tempted to refer to the subject which she was certain was at the forefront of her mind, though, Farran swallowed down that temptation. Quite clearly, as Georgia talked with her father about his day, she was doing her best to put yesterday's blow behind her. No good could come of reminding her of it every five minutes, Farran decided.

'If no one minds,' Henry Preston addressed his daughter and his stepdaughter as he pushed his pudding plate away, 'I'll get back to my workshop. I've a small problem to solve...' he muttered, and was still muttering as he left the table and ambled to the door.

I'll take him in a cup of coffee later, Farran thought fondly. Suddenly, though, she became conscious that as she was looking after her stepfather's disappearing back, Georgia was looking at her.

Quickly Farran switched her gaze to note the determined light in Georgia's blue eyes. She knew then that Georgia wanted her to do something. Something which— as on a few other occasions in the past—she knew she was not going to like.

She was certain of it when Georgia, catching herself observed, began, 'Farran...'

'No!' Farran cut her off, though only in jest because Georgia had had such dreadful traumatic news to come to terms with, and she knew she would do pretty well anything for her anyway.

'You haven't heard what it is yet!' Georgia smiled.

'I've got a nasty sort of feeling you're going to remedy that any minute now,' grinned Farran. Her grin faded as her stepsister got down to basics—and it was to be some while before it reappeared.

'The thing is,' Georgia began, 'that I went to see my solicitor today about contesting Aunty Hetty's last will.'

'Contesting it?' Farran exclaimed, realising with a jolt that quite plainly Georgia was not going to put the matter behind her as she had thought. Farran's heart sank—her memory of Stallard Beauchamp was that he was a man who would give no quarter if it came to a battle.

'Oh, don't worry, we're not going to be tossed around the law courts—it won't go that far,' Georgia told her. 'For one thing, we could never afford it if we lost the case, and since Stallard Beauchamp's loaded without Aunt Hetty's loot, and can easily afford to instruct the best barrister going, we'd probably lose anyway. I've...'

'Stallard Beauchamp's loaded?' Farran cut her off. 'How do you know he's loaded?'

'Everybody knows it, apparently—except us. According to my solicitor, he's *only* the big noise who runs the Deverill Group, that's all.'

'The Deverill Group?' Farran exclaimed in astonishment, 'You mean the financiers and bankers?' she gasped. 'The...'

'You've got it,' nodded Georgia, and went sailing on as though she had thought of nothing else all day, 'Which is why, since he can't possibly have a need for Aunt Hetty's fortune, and since you've met him before...' suddenly she hesitated, as though, having got to the crux of the matter, she was searching for the most tactful way to bring out the rest of it.

But already, from what Georgia had said so far, the hairs on the back of Farran's neck were beginning to prickle. She knew she was not going to like the answer, even as, the words seeming to be dragged from her, she reluctantly queried, 'What is it you want me to do?'

Georgia smiled, just as if she saw nothing at all wrong with the request she was about to make. 'I want you to go and see Stallard Beauchamp,' she said, and when, dumbstruck, Farran just sat and looked at her wide-eyed, 'I want you to point out to him that Aunt Hetty was our relative and not his, and say that, since he can't be in the need of her money when we are, would he please do the gentlemanly thing and rip up, burn, or just generally forget to present Aunt Hetty's last will to his solicitors, and agree to let her previous will stand.'

Farran's eyes were wider than ever when her stepsister came to an end. 'You're—not serious?' she questioned faintly.

'Oh, but I am,' Georgia replied.

Farran was still trying to talk her out of the idea at breakfast the next morning. 'But you've never met him!' she protested, having used every argument she could think of the previous evening. 'You've no idea what he's like!'

'He's a man, isn't he?' Georgia replied. 'A bachelor too, who, while he never looks like settling down, is—I discovered from a few phone calls I made when I left my solicitors—a man who according to popular rumour, while dodging all efforts to tie him down, has an eye for a beautiful woman.'

'You go and see him, then,' Farran said quickly. 'You're beautiful, and...'

'My beauty is the bottle and brush variety.' Georgia had an answer for that too. 'Your beauty's natural,' she went on. 'You look good without make-up, while I—

I'm not fit to be seen until I've spent half an hour in front of the dressing-table mirror.'

'You exaggerate,' Farran said gloomily, inwardly sensing that she was going to end up doing as Georgia asked, but still trying to get out of it.

'You'll get a third of the estate, too, if he agrees to let the previous will stand,' Georgia pressed.

'Huh!' Farran retorted, without the least sign of enthusiasm.

'I don't know how you can be like this,' Georgia brought more pressure to bear. 'I've told you of my plans to expand. And you know how Dad has set his heart on that lathe.' Squirming uncomfortably, Farran recalled again how not once had Georgia or her father ever thrown back at her how they had given her a home when her mother had walked out. She knew she was weakening rapidly when the idea struck her that perhaps this was a chance to repay their generosity. 'How can I go myself?' Georgia tried another tack. 'Linda and Christy are still off sick. You know how hard I slave at the salon. If you were working or were even half as busy as me it . . .'

'What the heck do I say to him?' All at once Farran caved in. 'How do I get started? What . . .'

'You'll think of something,' beamed Georgia, and before Farran could change her mind she fished inside her handbag. 'I've made a note of his office number,' she told Farran, passing a slip of paper over to her. 'I reckon that if you ring him at about half-past nine . . .'

Farran did not feel any more cheerful after Georgia had left to go to her business. Half-past nine came and went, however, before she realised that if she didn't get a move on her stepsister would be on the phone to ask how her call had gone before she had so much as phoned the Deverill Group offices.

A minute later Farran had taken a grip on herself and, although she was beginning to feel that she had been bulldozed into this, she dialled the number Georgia had given her.

'Ringing for you,' the switchboard operator at Deverill's said when she asked for Mr Beauchamp. Farran's mind then went a total blank.

She was clutching on to the phone for dear life when the ringing tone stopped, and a serene female voice said, 'Diana King.'

'Ah...' said Farran, ridiculously, she realised, as something occurred to her.

'Mr Beauchamp's secretary.' The serene voice attempted to get more from the caller than 'Ah'.

Another minute later, her efforts to speak with Stallard Beauchamp most politely blocked, Farran, having left her name and phone number in order that Mr Beauchamp could ring her back when he was 'available', replaced her receiver. One thing was by then fairly certain to her. If Diana King was married, then she must be the Mrs King who, under Stallard Beauchamp's direction, had made all the arrangements necessary for Miss Newbold's funeral.

The nerve of the man! To take it upon himself to instruct his secretary so! He might well have known by then that he was the sole beneficiary under Aunt Hetty's will, but what right did that give him over her family when it came to a thing like her funeral?

A few seconds later Farran's sense of fairness came back. Since none of Aunt Hetty's family had been near her for nigh on twelve months, she supposed he could be forgiven for thinking that, since they had shown no interest in her when she was alive, they would show no interest in her now that she was dead.

At that juncture the telephone rang. Nervously, knowing that she had thought of nothing with which to start her conversation with Stallard Beauchamp, but hoping to get his agreement to her request without the need to have to go and see him, Farran picked up the phone. 'Hello,' she said.

'How did you get on?' Georgia asked eagerly.

'He wasn't available. He's going to ring back,' Farran told her.

When morning rolled into afternoon with the phone staying silent, Farran was beginning to doubt that he would ring. Swine! she berated him again. Mrs King was sure to have given him her message that she would like to speak to him by now!

Poor Georgia, Farran was thinking when four o'clock came and went. Georgia must be on the same tenterhooks as herself, but, accepting that she would ring her the moment she heard from *him*, she had not rung again since that first phone call.

At half-past four Farran got fed up with looking at her watch. Then it was five and still no return call from Stallard Beauchamp. Knowing that Georgia would badger away at her that night for her to put through another call to the Deverill Group offices tomorrow, Farran began to hate him. She hadn't wanted to ring him today, she certainly did not want to ring him again tomorrow—and yet she was in debt to both Georgia and her father for their goodness.

At half-past five Farran knew he was not going to ring. When at six o'clock the phone did ring, she knew it was Georgia, the waiting too much for her.

'Hello,' she said, picking up the receiver.

'What did you want?' asked a tough-sounding voice which she had no trouble whatsoever in recognising.

'Oh, you got my message,' she waffled, her mind suddenly a blank. Plainly, though, Stallard Beauchamp had no time for wafflers; he made no reply, that alone giving her the impression that in another few seconds his receiver was going to be put down. 'Actually,' she said quickly to forestall that action, but finding it as impossible as she had thought it would be to ask what she had to ask and expect to receive a favourable reply, 'the thing is,' she invented on the spot, 'that I didn't—er—manage to take a note of the date of Miss Newbold's last will, and I was—er—wondering if maybe you could tell me?'

'Didn't you instruct your lawyer to get you a copy?' was the drawled sardonic reply, and Farran no longer wondered why some women went around hitting *some* men.

'I haven't seen my lawyer!' she retorted sharply.

'For a woman who's never heard of me, it didn't take long for you to find out from someone where to contact me, though, did it?' he tossed back at her witheringly.

'I didn't need to consult a lawyer to find that out. You're more well-known than you think!' Farran informed him.

'Obviously,' he murmured, and there was that note of mockery in his voice that caught her on the raw.

'Well,' she exploded, 'may I have the date of that will?' To her utter chagrin, Stallard Beauchamp had never heard of subterfuge, or if he had, he quite clearly did not care for it.

'You know the date!' he rapped, all mockery gone. 'Now, give me the true reason for your call!'

Damn him! Farran fumed, hating him as she had never hated anyone. Yet still she could not give him the true reason for her call. 'I—have a—a proposition to put to you,' was the best she could come up with, and promptly came within an ace of slamming the phone down on him when, with his mockery soon back, she heard his reply.

'My dear,' he startled her by drawling, 'I hardly know you!' And, while she was gasping at that, 'Are you in the habit of propositioning men on so brief an acquaintance?'

Farran took a deep and steadying breath, and through clenched teeth she hissed, 'Is there any point in my talking to you?'

'If you can be truthful, there might be,' he replied briskly.

At that instant she heard the sound of Georgia's car on the drive and, realising that her stepsister had made every effort to come home earlier, she had to grab at the carrot of 'there might be' which Stallard Beauchamp had just dangled.

'I want...' she began, when abruptly he interrupted her.

'I've calls queueing up for me,' he stated, and went on to inform her, 'I intend having something to eat at my club before I go home tonight. We'll discuss what you want—and what I might consider giving—over a meal.' He paused to give her the name and address of his club, and while Farran was still coming up for air at his high-handedness, 'I'll see you there in two hours,' he told her—and rang off.

Farran still had the phone in her hand when Georgia came looking for her. 'He's just rung?' she quickly put two and two together as she saw the receiver in Farran's hand and observed her stormy expression.

'He wants me to meet him—in two hours!' Farran erupted as she replaced the receiver.

'Where?' asked Georgia, a pleased look on her face.

'In London,' Farran told her, and went on to tell her how, lying all the way, she had ended up telling him that she had a proposition to put to him—and how he had called her bluff.

'You'd better wear something special,' Georgia declared the moment she had finished.

'I can't possibly go!' Farran objected.

'Of course you can,' Georgia overruled her. 'By virtue of the fact that Stallard Beauchamp has agreed to see you, it's plain that he's interested.'

Not in me, Farran thought, but in making me squirm. 'But even supposing I had a proposition to put to him—which I don't—I'll never make it in two hours!'

'You won't be too late if you take my car,' Georgia squashed all protests. 'My car's faster than Dad's. Come on, you can have a quick shower while I root around in your wardrobe. Just be glad,' she said lightly as they went towards the staircase, 'that it doesn't take you the half-hour it takes me to put on your warpaint!'

In less time than she would have considered likely, Farran was out of her trousers and sweater, showered and dressed in a sophisticated black light wool number. She wore no jewellery, and needed none, as, at Georgia's bidding, she put her foot down on the accelerator.

Mercifully she was an excellent driver, and she arrived at the discreet address, as her stepsister had said, not too late.

All the same, she would not have been surprised had she arrived just as Stallard Beauchamp was considering what to have for dessert. But no sooner had she adopted a mantle of being cool and unflappable and entered the élite gentlemen's club than her host appeared, not from the dining-room but from one of the other rooms.

He was as tall as she remembered him, and was immaculately turned out in his business suit, and—from nerves only, she realised—her insides did a little somersault at the sight of him. Moving easily with long strides, he came over to where she stood.

Unspeaking, he halted in front of her, his grey eyes taking in her tall, slender shape and moving over her elegant appearance from the top of her shiny dark brown hair to the tips of her black two-and-a-half-inch-heeled shoes.

For a brief instant she thought she glimpsed a glimmer of admiration in his eyes as he looked at her. But when she again flicked a glance up at him, she knew herself wrong, for as he murmured suavely, 'Hello, Farran,' the only look she could see in his eyes was one of cool courtesy.

CHAPTER THREE

'I'm sorry I'm late,' Farran began as, with a hand beneath her elbow, Stallard Beauchamp guided her across the reception area. She saw him slant a raised-eyebrowed look at her, and inwardly she cringed. Her apology had been made from an attempt to be as courteous as him, and not, as she was sure he believed, from any desire to ingratiate herself with him. 'I wasn't trying to creep!' she stiffly set the record straight as they reached the door of the dining-room.

'I didn't for a moment think you were,' he replied smoothly, and as the head waiter saw them and started to approach, 'Perhaps it's I who should apologise.'

'You?' she exclaimed, startled, having from the very first formed the view that he was a man who never apologised for anything.

'Me,' he answered evenly. 'For underestimating the time it would take you to get here from Banford.'

It was Farran's turn to send him a quick sideways look—apparently he knew where she lived! She might well have asked him how he knew, but her host was by then talking to the head waiter, who led the way to a table. She was then glad she had not put the question, because, as a chair was pulled out for her, she realised that the answer to how Stallard Beauchamp knew where she lived was quite simple. Aunt Hetty's previous will was in his possession—the address of her stepsister, stepfather and herself must, since that will was in their favour, be noted there.

Wishing that the meal was over before it had begun, Farran studied the menu as though she had an appetite, and chose mushroom soup with salmon *en croûte* to follow.

'Have you a preference for wine?' Stallard Beauchamp enquired courteously, although, since she suspected that one had to keep a very clear head when dealing with him, she would have preferred that the meal be wine-free.

However, since she was wary of him and had a rather uncomfortable feeling that he knew every thought that went through her head, she offered him a cool, if phoney, smile, and murmured, 'I'm driving, but perhaps a glass of something white might go down well.'

She was of the opinion that she had handled that rather well, but, as her soup arrived and the meal got under way, she knew that it was too early for self-congratulation.

If indeed self-congratulations were on the cards at all, she mused, because the only reason he had suggested they meet was so she could put her proposition to him. Since she did not *have* a proposition, all she could do was to bide her time until he brought the subject up. But, as the first course gave way to the second, it seemed to her that Stallard Beauchamp was intent on discussing every subject under the sun other than the one which she wanted brought up.

They were more than half-way through their main course when she suddenly began to form the most awful impression that Stallard Beauchamp was playing with her. At his instigation, they had discussed acid rain and air pollution, and she had had to dig deep to find an honest opinion on such issues. But, while the subjects he had chosen were worthy of debate, she was suddenly certain that he was merely playing with her, and knew perfectly well which other subject she really wanted to discuss.

She did not like at all the feeling that she was some puppet he was making dance to his tune, and she forgot to be cool for a moment and broke out hurriedly, 'Mr Beauchamp, I...' She halted, and was suddenly pinned by his unsmiling grey-eyed look.

Then, as she realised that she still wasn't ready, and began to doubt that she ever would be ready to plead with him to give up that which Miss Newbold must have wanted him to have—or she would not have willed it to him—all at once he looked solemnly back at her, and smiled.

'Stallard,' he said.

'What?' she queried, her brain power busy with trying to decide if his smile was genuine or not.

'How can I call you Farran if you insist on calling me Mr Beauchamp?' he patiently explained—something she seemed not to have the wit to sort out for herself.

Farran realised that it was time she pulled herself together. A lot depended on the outcome of this meeting; for Georgia's sake, and for Uncle Henry's sake, she could not allow her thoughts to go woolgathering.

'Stallard,' she smiled, and hoped he might have the same trouble in trying to decide whether her smile was genuine or not, although she somehow thought he wouldn't. 'This wine is lovely,' she complimented his choice, though the compliment was genuine, because it was a quite delicious wine.

'Talking of wine,' he looked up, 'did you manage to park without too much difficulty?' His eyes fastened on her lips as a genuine smile of amusement appeared on her beautiful mouth as the humour of him linking her comment about one glass of wine and driving amused her.

A matching genuine smile turned up the corners of his mouth too, and Farran experienced the most peculiar fluttering sensation as her eyes rested on his well-shaped mouth. 'I was lucky, I found a spot just outside,' she told him and, averting her gaze, for no good reason she found she was adding, 'I borrowed my stepsister's car.'

'You don't have a car of your own?' he enquired.

'I aim to get one soon,' she replied, and could have groaned out loud when a flicked look at him showed that his smile had gone and that, as if suspecting that she planned to use some of his inheritance on purchasing a new car, he was giving her a sharp scrutiny. Feeling damned if she'd explain how she had sold her car when she had gone to Hong Kong and how she had banked the proceeds with the intention of buying a different model when she returned, 'I have my own money!' she flared defiantly instead.

'So tell me,' Stallard Beauchamp said toughly, a steely look suddenly present in his eyes, 'why are you after mine?'

'I'm not!' she exploded, and when, at such a question, as far as she was concerned she would have leapt to her feet and got quickly out of there and away from the hateful brute, for Georgia's sake, and for Uncle Henry's sake, she had to stay there.

She hated Stallard Beauchamp worse than ever as, giving her a straight look, he coolly and loftily let fall, 'Aren't you?' Wanting with all she had to storm at him 'No, I'm jolly well not!', she was forced, because of what she was there to try to achieve, to sit and squirm. 'Perhaps, Farran,' Stallard, his tone quietly mocking, went on when she had not answered, 'you should tell me why you're here—and what it is that you want.'

'I want...' she began in a hurried rush to get it all over, but abruptly she stopped. Silently she tried out in her head the words she wanted to say, but even unsaid, they sounded blunt, money-grabbing, and totally avaricious.

'Come, Farran,' he coaxed, needling her whether he knew it or not. 'From what I've seen of you so far, I wouldn't have said you were the shy type.'

'What are you implying?' she asked sharply.

'What would I be implying,' he countered, 'but that I didn't notice any reticence about you when, uninvited, you walked into one of the bedrooms in my house and, without so much as a by your leave, had the wardrobe doors open before anyone could stop you.'

'I didn't know then that the house belonged to you— that it had been left to you!' Farran defended hotly.

'But you wish it was otherwise?'

'Naturally I do!' she told him vehemently, and as the waiter came to their table to ask them what they would like for their final course, she grabbed at the few minutes that afforded her to try and recapture some of her more normal poise.

By chance, both she and Stallard opted for cheese and biscuits—about the only thing they agreed on, she thought irritably. She flicked a glance at him and in the few seconds that he silently held her glance she realised it was crunch time. He had asked her once what it was that she wanted, and she knew then that he would not ask again. If there was anything that she wanted—and he knew full well that she would not have driven to see him if there wasn't—then it was up to her to tell him, and tell him now!

'Mr Beauchamp—St—Stallard...' she began, the two minutes she had just spent in composing herself an utter waste of time.

'Miss Henderson—Farran,' he replied, a light of devilment suddenly there in his eyes.

'You asked me what I wanted,' she gritted her teeth to tell him bluntly. 'Well, what I want is...' Her voice petered out as the urge to tell him to stuff his inheritance fought a battle royal against having to tell her dear stepsister when she got home how she had thrown away any chance she had of that money because of her pride. 'I wanted——' she began again, finding that pride was an almost insurmountable obstacle, 'that is, I wondered,' she pressed on when there was no help coming from him, 'I wondered—since you don't need the money...'

'You *have* been checking up on me,' he inserted drily.

'And since you weren't a relative of Miss Newbold,' Farran, now that she had got started, ploughed doggedly on, 'I wondered if you'd consider returning her estate to her rightful heirs?'

'Rightful heirs?' he queried, giving her a straight look as though to say what could be more rightful than a legally drawn-up, properly signed and witnessed will made out in his favour.

'You know what I mean!' Farran exclaimed shortly, finding that this man had the most uncanny knack of straining her temper.

'I'm sure I do,' he drawled. 'Correct me if I'm wrong, or if my hearing has been at fault, but have you—a non-relative yourself, as far as I can ascertain—just asked me to give up my claim—my rightful claim—to Miss Newbold's estate!'

My stars, was there ever such a man! Coming very near to exploding again, Farran stamped hard on the fury this man so easily aroused in her. Apart from that snide crack about her too being a non-relative, she was growing doubly positive that the hateful brute was playing her along for his own amusement.

How she managed to stay seated just then she could not have said, but, 'Yes,' she told him tersely, 'that's what I'm asking.' Still trying for calm, she observed his considering look as he steadily scrutinised her. 'Well?'

she enquired, only wanting him to say 'No' when, not waiting for coffee, she would be off.

'I'm thinking about it,' he replied, and smiled that insincere smile she had seen before. Then, his thinking done, but that insincere smile still there, 'Tell me, Farran, what is it you propose to give in exchange?' he enquired silkily.

It was his silky tone that did it. 'Not what you've got in mind!' she erupted hot-temperedly.

Abruptly his smile fell away, as did his silky tone as he wasted no time in setting her straight. 'You can have no possible idea of what's in my mind!' he told her shortly, and added bluntly, 'But—at the risk of offending—having a woman handed to me on a plate has never appealed.'

'Blast you, Stallard Beauchamp!' Farran exploded, totally infuriated by the odious, obnoxious creature. 'You'd be damn lucky! Apart from the fact that I'm off men for the duration...'

'Were I interested, I might ask why,' he sliced in, 'but since I'm not...'

'I wouldn't dream of telling you anyway!' Farran refused to let him get away with it.

'Since I'm not interested,' he ignored what she was saying to repeat, 'are you seriously telling me that you angled for me to invite you to dine...'

'Angled!' she exploded, but she was again ignored as that one word was all he allowed her.

'Angled for an invitation to dine, with no more to back you than that you want me to give up my inheritance!'

'It was certainly never in my mind to go to bed with you to get it!' Farran shot in before he could draw breath, and, not giving him a chance to derisively state yet again that he liked to do his own hunting, she went on, 'But in any case, it's not your inheritance, it's...' Suddenly her voice faded.

'It isn't?'

'Well...' she said lamely, then found strength to bluff, 'Well, it might be now, but once the wheels have been set in motion to contest the will...'

'Ah!' he cut in. 'So you're going to contest the will?' He pinned her with a mocking grey-eyed look, and Farran knew at that point that she had tried to bluff the wrong man and that her bluff was about to be called. 'May I wish you all luck in your endeavours,' he smiled that smile she was beginning to hate as much as she hated him. Especially did she hate him when, his tone conveying that she was going to need all the luck she could get, he went on, 'I'm sure the judge will be most impressed when you tell him how, in the last year of Miss Newbold's life, in the year of her failing health, not once did you visit her; or even so much as pick up the phone for a loving chat.'

Farran did not like this man heaping guilt at her and her family's door. But, feeling unable to defend her family—because Stallard Beauchamp would never understand about her stepfather's vagueness about anything except his inventions, nor would he, a man who worked an overstretched business day himself, ever understand about Georgia being too busy with her business to visit her elderly relative—she was left trying to defend herself.

'I told you—I was in Hong Kong!' she protested, starting to get annoyed again by this man and the fact that she was actually defending herself to him!

'So you did,' he acknowledged, and went on cynically, 'I'm sure His Honour will find it most enlightening when he hears that, although you couldn't find the time to leave Hong Kong when Miss Newbold was so ill, you no sooner heard that the dear soul had passed away than you were on the next plane home.'

'It wasn't like that!' Farran flared. 'I've already told you, I didn't know she'd died until after I'd given up my job and flown home!'

Stallard Beauchamp shrugged. 'Really?' he replied, but it was more in the nature of a sarcastic comment than a question.

'Yes, really!' Farran answered him shortly just the same. 'I liked Miss Newbold. I was fond of her—I wrote to her several times while I was away.'

'You thought that was all you needed to do to get your avaricious little hands on her money!'

'No!' she told him sharply. 'I never gave her money nor her will a thought!' Lord, how she loathed this detestable man! Though it was more to set him right than an attempt to exonerate herself in his eyes that she charged on, 'I wrote to her because I did, that's all! I just happen to get on with elderly people,' she told him, 'and *that* is a pure and honest fact!' With that, and with her eyes spitting fury, she reached for her bag, looking straight into his cool grey eyes. 'My family has much more right to everything that was willed to you, and you know it!' She was on her feet when she hissed, 'I hope you sleep easy in your bed when you've claimed what's rightfully my...'

'I haven't yet said that I intend to claim anything,' Stallard Beauchamp cut in idly. And when, silenced and staring, Farran stood looking at him, he added mockingly, 'To coin a phrase—stick around, you may hear something to your advantage—and to the advantage of the other previous co-legatees.'

For all of five seconds Farran remained staring at him. On the one hand she had more than enough of Stallard Beauchamp and his cat-and-mouse games. On the other hand, with him using the word 'advantage' and in the same breath the words 'previous co-legatees'—surely, for the sake of her step-family, she could put up with the insufferable man for a few minutes longer? With some reluctance she sat down again.

If she had learned anything in this last trying hour, though, it was that she would do well not to underestimate the man opposite her. That being so, she saw no point in pussyfooting around. Tact was a thing of the past, as she said bluntly, 'You intimated that you might not claim what's been left to you. But I can't see you giving up what's been willed to you from some philanthropic feeling.'

At that juncture coffee was brought to their table. 'How right you are,' Stallard Beauchamp agreed when the waiter had gone. 'I've had an idea,' he told her pleasantly—his very pleasantness, without her knowing what his idea was, enough to make her wary. 'An idea which would probably not have occurred to me,' he went on, 'had you not recently mentioned that, as well as being without a job at present, you also happen to "purely and honestly" get on with elderly people.'

Startled by what he was saying, Farran set her normally quick-thinking brain to work. 'You've—some idea of my working in an old people's home?' she questioned, this seeming to be the only logical answer that would fit.

Being so certain that her deductions were way off beam, however, she was totally staggered when Stallard agreed, 'Something like that,' and when she stared at him wide-eyed, 'Though in actual fact, it's not an old people's home, but the home of an aged lady.'

'You—want me to work for an elderly person?' she checked. He nodded. 'As her secretary?' she questioned, adding, 'You know I'm a secretary,' not liking the sound of his idea before he went any further.

This time, though, he shook his head. 'Your secretarial skills won't be needed,' he told her, 'just your
talent for getting on well with the elderly. Miss Irvine's
companion has just walked out on her,' he went on
smoothly, 'and she's in need of a temporary companion
while I look round for someone more tolerant than her
last one.'

'Miss Irvine?' queried Farran, having no wish whatsoever to be companion to her, whoever she was.

'You may remember seeing her at Miss Newbold's funeral,' he obliged.

All Farran's instincts were suddenly ominously at
work. 'The lady with the hat?' she guessed. 'The hat
with the...'

'The ostrich feather,' Stallard took up, and as Farran
remembered unhesitatingly how disagreeable the woman
had looked, she knew that, even for her stepsister, there
was no way she was going to take on the absurd job.

'Is she a relation of yours?' she queried, as she remembered thinking how, with him looking as sour as
the lady she now knew to be Miss Irvine, she had thought
that somehow they must be related.

Just as though he knew what she was thinking, Stallard
gave her a suspicious look. Sweetly Farran smiled, and
saw from the way his eyes narrowed that he did not care
for her phoney smiles any more than she cared for his.
Looking away from him, she drained the last of her
coffee, and was coldly informed, 'Miss Irvine is a—
family friend.'

With friends like that, who needs enemies? Farran
thought, and, her meal over, and this conversation over
too as far as she was concerned, she reached for her bag
a second time, and for a second time she stood up. This
time Stallard stood up too, and as, like the good-
mannered person she was, she politely thanked him for
the meal, he escorted her from the dining-room.

'I'll walk with you to your car,' he told her smoothly when she turned at the door of the club to wish him a brief goodnight.

She was tall herself, but he was still a good deal taller. Russell, she recalled easily, was an inch or two shorter than her, but that didn't matter. She... Hastily she pushed Russell from her mind, as she and Stallard Beauchamp reached the spot where she had parked the car.

'Goodnight,' she said coolly as she unlocked it and got behind the wheel.

'Ring me at home tomorrow night,' Stallard instructed, slipping his personal card into her right hand before she could close the door. 'By then,' he paused to have the last infuriating word, 'I'll have broken the news to Miss Irvine that she'll have to put up with you for a while.'

Farran pulled the driver's door to, hard, wishing his fingers were still in the way. But he was standing back from the car, his hands well out of harm's way. 'You'll wait a hell of a long time if you wait for me to ring,' she muttered under her breath and, setting the car in motion, she roared away.

Thoughts of Stallard Beauchamp occupied her mind for most of her journey back to Banford. Him and his tormenting cat-and-mouse play! she fumed, one thought chasing furiously after another. First dangling the bait that he might be prepared to give up the money which had been willed to him, then, when he had discovered that she had no proposition to put to him, suggesting that she go and work for that—that tartar!

Tartar was the right word too, she realised as more miles sped by. For just then a picture came to her mind of a sour-looking woman disagreeably instructing an intense-looking woman to go and do something or other

at Miss Newbold's funeral. Without a doubt the intense
woman had been Miss Irvine's companion.

Farran arrived back in Banford having been through
every word and every look that had passed between her
and Stallard Beauchamp. She let herself into the house
knowing that she definitely did not want the job as companion to an elderly lady. And most emphatically, there
was no way she would voluntarily take up residence with
Miss Irvine—that most disagreeable-looking of all elderly ladies!

'Thank heavens you're back!' Georgia pounced on her
the moment she went through the door.

'What's happened?' Farran asked urgently, never
having seen her stepsister in such a state of anxiety.

'You tell me!' returned Georgia, and as she realised
that Georgia's anxiety stemmed solely from the agony
of waiting to hear how she had got on, Farran realised
that it was going to be more difficult to tell her than she
had thought.

'You're not going to like this,' she began as the two
of them went from the hall to the sitting-room. 'I...'

Georgia did not like it. To Farran's consternation,
though, it was not what Stallard Beauchamp had asked
her that she did not like, but the fact that she had no
intention of doing as he asked. Far from agreeing that
she could not possibly go and act as temporary companion to the disagreeable Miss Irving, Georgia could
see nothing wrong with the idea!

'But you *do* like old people,' she pointed out. 'And
you *are* good with them.'

'I know, but...'

'Nor do you have a job at the moment—and it would
be *only* temporary.'

'Yes, but...'

'Oh, Farran,' Georgia went on to coax, 'it is your inheritance as well as mine that we're talking of!'

'I know,' Farran replied, but before she could go on to say that, although she was not averse to receiving an inheritance, in her view the price she had to pay was too high, Georgia was cutting in to pile on more pressure.

'And if you're not bothered about the money for yourself, think about Dad, think about me. You know how much Dad wants that new lathe, and I don't need to tell you, surely, about the desperate situation I'm in.'

Farran went to bed that night in a most unhappy frame of mind. To be made to realise that she was being very selfish in her stubborn refusal to take on the job of temporary companion did not sit very well with her. As Georgia had pointed out, she did, as a rule, get on with elderly people, and as Georgia had said, she was at the moment without a job. Nor when repeating the conversation between her and Stallard Beauchamp had she, as Georgia was quick to seize upon, given him an outright 'No' when it came to *his* proposition.

Farran knew by the time she got up the next morning that, having weighed up all the pros and cons, what she personally did or did not want to do did not come into it. She loved both her stepfather and stepsister, and it was from that love, not a sense of duty, that she was left without a choice.

Particularly did she love her stepsister when, as the two met up at breakfast, Georgia's first words on looking at her were not a resumption of last night's pressures, but a gentle, unthought exclamation of, 'Oh, love, you've had a terrible night, haven't you!'

'Does it show?' Farran found a smile, and as they sat down to breakfast she realised that she did not want her stepsister to spend the whole of the day in deep anxiety about what she intended to do. 'I've decided to ring Stallard Beauchamp tonight,' she told her, and at the relieved beam of a smile that came to Georgia's face Farran knew she was committed.

'You won't regret it,' Georgia told her brightly.

Farran tried to keep that thought in the front of her mind throughout the rest of that day. How could she regret being instrumental in ultimately giving her stepfather purchasing power for the piece of equipment he wanted? How could she regret giving that same help to her stepsister?

When thoughts of either her stepfather, or her stepsister, and how much she owed them, were not filling her mind, Farran tried to get herself in a positive frame of mind. She *was* without work, wasn't she? She had known that some time soon she would have to start to look for a job. So, OK, she would soon have started looking for a secretarial job, but what was the difference—work was work, wasn't it?

Knowing that she was fooling no one but herself, Farran half wished her phone call was made and over with. It was galling to have to ring Stallard, especially when she rather thought she had given him the impression that he needn't stay in waiting for her to ring him—tonight or ever.

Having no idea if Stallard Beauchamp worked late, or finished early, for that matter, on a Friday, she decided to leave it until around eight that evening to make her call. She had thought, though, that, perhaps out of interest, or maybe just to give her moral backing, Georgia would stay in that night. But when Georgia arrived home it soon became apparent that, having every confidence that nothing could go wrong now, she was in a tremendous hurry to be off somewhere.

'It's my turn to go out to dinner tonight!' she greeted Farran happily.

You could have had my turn last night and welcome, Farran thought, though she was pleased to see Georgia so happy. 'Is he anyone I know?' she queried, having met several of her stepsister's men friends.

'I only met him myself this week,' Georgia smiled, and there was a pleasantly anticipatory look in her eyes as she revealed, 'His name's Idris Vaughan. He's the architect with whom I'll have to work very closely over the alterations I want.'

From the look of it, Farran thought her stepsister was quite smitten, but shortly after Georgia had gone out, Farran was back on the treadmill of the thoughts that had been with her all that day.

At a quarter to eight she could see absolutely no point in waiting another fifteen nerve-racking minutes for eight o'clock to arrive. Sighing deeply, she found the card Stallard Beauchamp had given her and went over to the telephone. Gritting her teeth, she dialled, and waited.

To her utmost chagrin, since she was sure she had given him the impression that she was not going to ring, Stallard Beauchamp sounded not the least surprised to hear her.

Swallowing down her wrath, Farran decided that since he could not have been all *that* sure that she would ring tonight, he would not have contacted Miss Irvine to, as he had put it last night, break the news that she would have to put up with her for a while. So she supposed she must still have been looking for an out when she asked him, 'Have you acquainted Miss Irvine with the fact that she's to have a new, but temporary, companion?'

'She knows,' Stallard Beauchamp drawled, making her grit her teeth again at his colossal confidence.

'She doesn't think that a twenty-three-year-old is too young for the position?' Farran asked, but when she realised that she must still have been looking for a way of escape, she immediately had to back-pedal when he asked her bluntly,

'Do you want the job or not?'

Swine! she fumed. 'How long is "temporary"?' she questioned in return.

'Three months,' he told her unhesitatingly.

That long! Her heart sank. About to snap that surely it wouldn't take him that long to find the right permanent companion, Farran remembered the disagreeable-looking Miss Irvine, and realised she was lucky. To her way of thinking, it could take all of six months to get someone suitable to put up with the sour old trout.

'And you agree that at the end of that time—the three months—you, in return, will destroy that will in your favour?'

'You have my word,' Stallard Beauchamp replied.

'You don't think I should have something in writing?' Farran pressed, and wanted to physically lash out at the loathsome man when, his tone arrogant, he answered sharply,

'I don't know what group of people you mix with, Miss Henderson, but in the circles I move in, my word is, and always has been, good enough.'

Feeling verbally slapped down, Farran hated him even more. Choking down her ire, 'Where does Miss Irvine live?' she asked him stonily, and, since she must have been a friend of Aunt Hetty's, 'Does she live in High Monkton t...'

'Miss Irvine lives in Low Monkton,' he cut in crisply, mentioning a village which Farran knew was about two miles down the road from Miss Newbold's home.

There seemed little more that she had to ask him after that, other than when she should start. To Farran's way of thinking, since she was committed, the sooner she began this wretched three-month marathon the sooner it would end.

'All being well, I can probably catch a train as far as Dorchester on Monday,' she told him, in the hope that he would take the hint that she was ready to start immediately.

She was infuriated once again though when, his tone as arrogant as ever, he promptly squashed any say she might have thought she had in the matter—or any idea on what she thought was immediate—by telling her, 'I'll call for you at ten tomorrow morning. Be packed and ready.' With that, his receiver went down.

Arrogant pig! she fumed. What if she had other arrangements for tomorrow? As she had sighed at the start of her phone call, Farran sighed again. She viewed the future bleakly. She had thought that nothing worse could happen than to find out that the man she loved and had looked up to was a man of cardboard—but she was beginning to wonder.

CHAPTER FOUR

FARRAN was lying wide awake when some time after midnight she heard Georgia arrive back from her date with Idris Vaughan. She was glad though when, regardless of the hour, Georgia, in happy spirits, thought to look in to see how her telephone call had gone. One look at her packed suitcases standing by the foot of the bed, however, was all she needed to know that there had been no last-minute hitch.

'When?' she asked.

'Tomorrow, at ten,' Farran replied, and saw from her expression that Georgia had not thought she would be starting her new job so soon either.

Georgia quickly recovered, however, and came to sit at the foot of her bed. 'Well, it's not a date with the executioner you have, love, so cheer up,' she urged. 'Now, what did he have to say?' she asked.

Henry Preston breakfasted with Farran and Georgia for once the next morning. Farran, with Georgia's full agreement, had decided that there was no point in telling him the ins and outs of what was happening. But, to cheer her, he seemed not to want her to go away again so soon when Farran gave him a sketchy outline of her plans.

'But you've only just come home!' he protested.

'I shall only be away for three months this time,' she smiled, and hoped her smile hid how unenthusiastically she viewed the coming three months.

Five minutes later he left the breakfast table, grumbling that he'd seen nothing of her since she'd been back.

To which Georgia, who was about the only one on top form that morning, turned to Farran to laugh, 'It's all your fault, of course. To hear him talk, you'd never know that he spends every spare minute in his workshop!' Again Farran found a smile, but her smile disappeared when her stepsister said seriously, 'Farran, I've been thinking, and it doesn't seem to me to be at all satisfactory from our point of view that all we've got as a guarantee that this Stallard Beauchamp will tear up Aunt Hetty's last will is his word that he'll destroy it when your three months are up.'

'I did suggest I should have something in writing...' Farran began.

'I know you did,' Georgia remembered from their conversation in the small hours. 'But I really do think you should insist.'

Georgia, Farran thought after she had left for her salon, really did not know anything about the type of man Stallard Beauchamp was if she thought that one could *insist* on anything where he was concerned!

Having taken her cases down into the hall shortly after breakfast, Farran was up in her room when as ten o'clock neared she heard the front door bell ring. There was no turning back now, and she knew it when, leaving her room, she had started to descend the stairs and saw that Mrs Fenner had answered the door and was inviting Stallard Beauchamp in.

He halted in the hall, and as he looked across and up at her Farran paused mid-stair. Then, as suddenly their eyes met and held, she was visited by a most unexpected feeling of breathlessness. For goodness' sake, don't be ridiculous! she scolded herself, and put that breathlessness down to nerves and the reluctance she felt to begin the task in front of her.

Dragging her eyes away from the tall, broad-shouldered look of him, she continued on her way down the stairs. At the bottom she paused again, but this time to exchange a word with Mrs Fenner who, in passing, and with her years of service giving her a special place in the household, asked her if she would be wanting coffee.

Silently blessing their 'treasure', Farran had too much refinement therefore not to feel obliged to observe certain courtesies in front of their housekeeper. Her eyes went again to Stallard.

'Would you like coffee before we set off?' she smiled and asked.

Stallard Beauchamp looked at her and held her glance, then he smiled too, a slow natural smile, a smile which, unlike hers, had nothing forced about it.

'We'll get on our way, Farran—if that's all right with you,' he said pleasantly, his good manners quite obviously every bit as saintly as hers.

Turning from him, she saw that Mrs Fenner had got that message, and she said goodbye to her. As Mrs Fenner disappeared in the direction of the kitchen, though, Farran began to wonder if good manners decreed that she should risk introducing Stallard to her stepfather.

'I'll just go and say goodbye to my stepfather,' she told him, explaining prettily, 'He'll be up to his ears in—er—sump oil,' she drew out of the hat, 'or I'd take you into his workshop to...'

'I don't mind a bit of sump oil,' Stallard replied evenly, only his eyes mocking her and seeming to know that she was nervous about something.

Blessing Stallard Beauchamp too, Farran led the way to the workshop. 'Uncle Henry!' she called to the back of the bent-over, off-white-overalled shape. Henry Preston turned round. He had a grease smear on his forehead, but he was otherwise presentable—it was early in the day yet. 'This is Stallard Beauchamp,' Farran went on, then hesitated. All of a sudden she knew that she should not have risked bringing him in here to introduce him. Somehow she had a feeling that Uncle Henry might object if he knew what she was about to do. 'Mr Beauchamp is my employer,' she went on. 'St—Stallard, my stepfather, Henry Preston,' she nervously completed the introduction. As Henry Preston inspected his right hand and, seeming to think it was up to muster, extended it to meet the extended right hand of the tall man whose alert grey eyes seemed to miss not a thing, she added quickly, 'We're going now.'

She was seated beside Stallard and they were driving away before she drew another easy breath. For Henry Preston had come with them to the drive and had waited while Stallard had stowed her cases in the boot, and had waited too to hear the engine fire before, with a wave of his hand, he had returned to his workshop.

Having just found release from one lot of tension, though, Farran tensed up again when, before they had been driving along for five minutes, Stallard commented, 'I'm curious.'

Swallowing down a pert, 'You know what that did to the cat', Farran queried, 'Oh?'

'I'm curious to know why, when he's going to benefit too, you haven't told your stepfather the full whys and wherefores of what you're about.'

'How do you know I haven't told him everything?' Farran attempted to bluff, forgetting for a moment that this man was a master at calling one's bluff.

'Have you?' he questioned directly.

Damn him! she fumed, not for the first time. Suddenly, though, she realised that since it was only her stepfather who she did not want to know the whys and wherefores of everything, there was no reason to pretend with the bluff-calling brute by her side.

'As a matter of fact, no,' she said shortly.

'Why?' he wanted to know.

'Because—well, because there's no special reason why he should know,' Farran, after a hesitant start, finished sharply—and for her sins drew the edge of Stallard's wrath.

'You're not seriously suggesting that, since what you're doing is so the three of you may inherit what you've waited so long for, he wouldn't approve of it?'

Cynical pig! Farran thought angrily, and tilted her chin an uppity fraction to tell him disdainfully, 'I'm not suggesting anything.'

'Your stepsister knows, though?' he questioned, slicing unremittingly straight through her efforts to freeze him off the subject.

Farran expelled an angry breath of annoyance. 'Yes!' she snapped. 'She does.'

'And your mother?'

Were her life not in his hands because he was driving, Farran would have felt sorely tempted to hit him on the head with her bag. But from somewhere she found some sort of control. 'What's my mother got to do with any of this?' she stormed. 'I haven't seen her since she walked out on Henry, Georgia and me when I was thirteen!'

Twice as angry with him that he had made her slip up and reveal something she found difficult to talk about with another living soul, Farran abruptly turned her head away and looked out of a side window.

All at once, though, he had her turning again, and staring at him. For the toughness with which he had so far questioned her was gone, and there was, to her surprise, a hint of gentleness in his tone as, he mocked quietly, 'I knew if we looked hard enough we'd find we had something in common.'

'You...' she began, then brought out the only thing that would fit. 'Your mother left home too?'

'When I was but a babe,' he replied, but didn't look as though it bothered him in any way.

Wondering how his mother's leaving him, and presumably leaving his father too, had affected him, Farran, with her natural sensitivity, would have made some gentle enquiry. Just in time, though, she recalled what a swine this man was to her, so she swiftly swallowed down her sensitivity and told him waspishly instead, 'If I liked you I might feel sorry for you.'

'If I liked you, I might care,' he tossed back at her before she could blink. And suddenly they were both—laughing!

Turning her head away as his laughter faded, Farran thought that with Stallard in a good humour there was no better time than now to bring up the subject which had to be brought up before they went any further.

'I've been thinking,' she said, without stopping to think, and unconsciously paraphrasing her stepsister's words, 'that, from my point of view, it isn't very satisfactory that all I've got as a guarantee that you'll destroy that last will is your word.'

It did not take long for Stallard Beauchamp to swing from being good-humoured to being a bad-tempered, disgruntled brute, Farran discovered swiftly. For her words were barely out of her mouth than, 'Damn your impudence!' he snarled in a tone there was no arguing with. 'My word is all you're getting!'

Wishing with all she had that she was in a position to demand that he turn the car around this minute and take her straight back to Banford, Farran sent a barrowload of hate vibes his way and stared out through the windscreen.

Detestable, loathsome reptile! she labelled him, and determined that never, ever again would she speak to him. Though, since he did not seem to be falling over himself to converse with her, she did not find that any trouble.

His expression, she observed, when she turned slightly and caught a glimpse of it, was not conducive to her wanting to break the silence anyhow. For as they covered mile after mile, his expression barely altered from being stony and forbidding.

Not that she cared. Although, having travelled on this road before, when she saw signs that it would not be long now before they reached Low Monkton, Farran realised that she would have to talk to the pig of a man, if only to find out what was expected of her in this new job.

'What do I have to do?' she blurted out coldly—no time like the present.

'Do?' he questioned shortly. 'What do you mean, "do"?'

Give me strength, she prayed. 'What,' she clipped, 'will be my precise duties as a companion?'

'How the hell do I know?' he snarled for her pains.

'You're my employer—you damn well should know!' she had the joy of wrong-footing him. He ignored her.

Silence reigned in the car as she simmered and he continued to look disgruntled. Then, silkily, he was drawling, 'For an employee, you've already slipped up very badly.'

'How?' she snapped.

'You haven't asked how much I'm going to pay you yet.'

'I don't want your money!' she flared.

'You surprise me,' he lobbed at her sardonically, and Farran no longer wondered how wars began.

'So I'll have a hundred pounds a week all found,' she erupted. 'And that,' she added nastily, as she remembered the sour Miss Irvine, 'will be cheap at the price.'

To her discomfiture, he replied, 'Done!'

They were at Miss Irvine's door before either of them spoke again. 'Has Miss Irvine any health problems I should know about?' Farran felt she could do no other then enquire.

'She has a little arthritis in one shoulder, but generally, she's quite well,' Stallard informed her.

Farran took what she considered her last breath of freedom as Stallard rang the bell of the larger than average detached house and they waited for Miss Irvine to answer it.

'Stallard!' she greeted him as though pleased to see him when at last she came to the door.

'Hello, Nona,' he replied, his tone warmer than any tone Farran had heard him use on her. 'I've brought Farran to stay with you for a while,' he told her and, as they stepped inside the hall and the elderly lady who, although she had a pleasant look for him, favoured her new companion with a look that was more severe than pleasant, Stallard performed the introductions.

'Stallard said on the phone that you had family connections with Hetty Newbold,' Nona Irvine commented as she led the way to her velvet-chaired, velvet-curtained sitting-room. 'I think I remember you at her funeral,' she added as she sat her tall but plump form down on an amber velvet-covered chair and invited the other two to be seated. 'I'm sure you could both do with a cup of coffee after your drive,' she went on elegantly. 'I'll make it presently.'

'I'll do it.' Stallard took the words out of Farran's mouth. 'I'll leave you to get to know each other,' he murmured, to Farran's ears sounding more high and mighty than diplomatic as he disappeared.

All trace of being in any way pleasant dropped away from Nona Irvine once he had gone, however, and she looked every bit as disagreeable as Farran remembered her. 'Have you ever been a companion to anyone before?' she asked sharply.

Wondering how much Stallard had or had not told Miss Irvine, and whether perhaps since she was a friend of his family she knew the contents of Aunt Hetty's will, all Farran could do was play it by ear.

'I'm a trained secretary,' she told her politely, and keeping her glance on the lined features of the once good-looking woman, she added, 'I thought I'd like to take a brief holiday from secretarial work.'

'You think being a companion to me will be a holiday?' Miss Irvine asked sharply.

'I'm sure it won't be!' Farran, without thinking, returned smartly.

It was then that she realised two things—one, that the elderly lady knew nothing of Miss Newbold's affairs and how she had left them, or she would not have hesitated to scorn that she merely fancied a change from secretarial work. The other thing she realised, as Miss Irvine's face cracked and her mouth turned upwards at her smart reply, was that she had a sense of humour!

'Have you any idea what your duties will be?' Nona Irvine went on to ask as her face resumed its more normal crabbed lines.

'I'm hoping you'll tell me,' Farran replied evenly.

'You do play bridge, of course.'

'I'm afraid I don't,' she was forced to confess, and received a black look for her trouble.

'You can *drive*, I hope?' Miss Irvine questioned disagreeably.

'Yes—but I haven't a car.'

'There's one in the garage. Stallard bought it for me when that Titmarsh woman—your predecessor,' she sniffed, 'said we needed one to get out and about in.' Farran begrudgingly thought Stallard was most generous to buy the crusty old dear a car, but he went promptly from her mind when Miss Irvine proceeded to give her a third-degree on why she did not play bridge. Farran was fast forming the view that it was Miss Irvine's belief that a person could not be right in the head if they did not enjoy a good game of cards, when, Stallard returned, bearing the coffee.

Miss Irvine, Farran was soon to discover, was at her best when he was in view. 'How's your week gone?' he asked her as the three of them sat drinking coffee.

'Oh, very well, thank you, Stallard,' she replied.

'Any problems?' he enquired, from which Farran gleaned that had there been, he would at once have sorted them out. It seemed, she thought, that it was important to Stallard Beauchamp that Miss Irvine's remaining years were trouble-free.

'No problems at all.' Her face cracked into a smile again. 'Well, no problem,' she went on, 'that couldn't be solved if someone could teach Joan Jessop that a two-club opening means twenty-three points and that she's just *not allowed* to say "no bid" in reply.'

'Joan Jessop's your new bridge partner?' Stallard queried, and as Miss Irvine agreed that she was Farran was able to work out that Aunt Hetty must have been Nona Irvine's previous bridge partner, and that Stallard must have somehow met Aunt Hetty through that connection.

During the next half-hour, conversation flowed amicably in the sitting-room of Miss Irvine's home. Farran took part in the conversation whenever some comment included her. She was able to see clearly in that half-hour, though, that not only did Stallard have a lot of time for the elderly lady, but that he regarded her more as family than the family friend which he had told her Miss Irvine was.

That he was a regular visitor to the house at Low Monkton was plain too, as Farran learned that he had an open invitation to stay the weekend whenever he chose—although to date, it seemed, he had never availed himself of that overnight invitation. Nor was he going to avail himself of it this weekend, Farran heard, with some relief.

'I don't suppose I can press you to stay?' Miss Irvine queried when, at the end of that half-hour, he stood up, saying he would bring Farran's cases in.

'I've arrangements made for this evening,' he smiled.

'Who's the lucky woman tonight?' Miss Irvine asked with, to Farran's surprise, a look of teasing in her faded blue eyes.

Farran caught the glance Stallard sent her, and so that he should know she didn't think much of his poor date's luck, whoever she was, she cast her eyes heavenward—then almost dropped with shock, for she could have sworn that as she flicked her glance back to him he was on the brink of breaking out into a grin.

He did not break out into a grin, of course, but went abruptly from the sitting-room and out to his car. When he returned he had a large suitcase in each hand.

'Which room is Farran having?' he enquired of Nona Irvine.

'The one nearest the top of the stairs,' she answered, but added quickly, 'If you leave her cases in the hall, Farran can go up later.'

'It will limit the risk of accidents if I show her up now,' he replied smoothly, and Farran realised that that was his tactful way of saying it would save Miss Irvine's legs if he showed Farran her room.

Leaving her chair Farran accompanied him from the sitting-room. At the bottom of the stairs he stood back so that she should go first. At the top of the stairs she halted at the first bedroom door she came to. 'This one?' she asked, and waited politely while he nodded and pushed the door open.

Surprise awaited both of them as they went in, however, for the room still bore traces of its previous occupant. Though Farran was surprised on another count when, glancing at the spilled powder and dust-smeared dressing-table, Stallard Beauchamp actually apologised.

'Sorry about this!' he exclaimed. 'Miss Titmarsh, Nona's ex-companion, walked out last Wednesday. I—mistakenly it seems—thought Nona's cleaning woman came Mondays, Wednesdays and Fridays.' Briefly he paused. Then, 'We'll find you another room,' he declared promptly.

But Farran did not intend to start off with the mistress of the house on totally the wrong foot. That dear lady quite plainly wanted her to have this room and would not take at all kindly to her availing herself of another inside an hour of starting her new job.

'Contrary to your obvious belief that I've never so much as held a duster in my hands,' Farran swiftly halted him before he could take her cases to another room, 'and at the risk of ruining your opinion of me, I promise you it won't take me long to lick this room into shape.'

He did not like her sarcastic tone, she could tell that. But it did have the desired effect, she saw, in that, after affording her a particularly dark look, he thumped her cases down on the carpet. Farran smiled sweetly.

She was not smiling sweetly for long, however, because, before he went striding from the room, he dipped his hand into his pocket and withdrew a cheque, which she later realised he must have made out while he was waiting for the coffee he'd made to brew.

'Your first month's salary,' he said grittily as he pushed the cheque into her hands. And, affording her an insincere smile, 'I do so hope you're made to earn it,' he drawled, and left her staring after him.

* * *

Within a very short time of beginning her job of companion in earnest, Farran was discovering what very hard work it was. Apart from constantly trying to be agreeable to a tartar who seemed intent on being constantly disagreeable, she had barely a minute to call her own.

Although she had found that there was a genteel side to Miss Irvine, inside twenty-four hours she felt no surprise that Miss Titmarsh had walked out on her. Nor was it any wonder to her that when she had left, her room should be so untidy. The wonder, Farran thought when she went to bed on Sunday night, would have been if Miss Titmarsh had ever found time to tidy it!

Farran got out of bed on Monday morning and resolved that nothing was going to get her down that day. As well as being companion, she was also, she had learned, part-time cook.

She was busy in the kitchen making the porridge which Miss Irvine liked to start her day with in preference to anything else, when Miss Irvine came to inspect what she was doing.

'Make sure there aren't any lumps in it,' she ordered. 'There were lumps in it yesterday,' she complained.

Farran knew full well that there had not been any lumps in her previous day's efforts, but visions of the newspaper headlines if she emptied the saucepan's contents over the 'sweet old lady's' head saw her striving hard to remember just why she had agreed to do this job.

'Did you sleep well?' she asked, again resolving to make the best of things.

'I never sleep well,' Miss Irvine snapped. Farran stirred the porridge.

They were both seated at the breakfast table when, trying to be 'companionable', Farran remarked pleasantly, 'Stallard said something about your cleaning lady coming three days a week. Is this one of her days?'

Looking across at her, though, she was a little taken aback to observe what she could only describe as a look of guilt in the faded blue eyes that would not quite meet her own.

'Can't *you* handle a vacuum cleaner?' Nona Irvine asked a touch irritably.

Farran could, easily, but she sensed that there were a few questions to be asked here. 'I can,' she told Miss Irvine, 'but is there any reason why I should?'

'We'll be up to our ears in dirt by the weekend if you don't,' the elderly lady responded and, the guilt gone, added, 'I dismissed Mrs Lunn for insolence last Friday.'

'Insolence?' Farran queried.

'She had the sauce to call me a nagging old bitch! What do you think of that?'

Don't tempt me, thought Farran, and added 'domestic' to her 'part-time cook' duties, while in between she endeavoured to be a good companion to a body who would try the patience of a saint.

Tuesday was a bridge day. That was to say, they had lunch early so that Farran could drive Miss Irvine to Joan Jessop's home to begin a two o'clock bridge session.

'You can have the afternoon off,' Miss Irvine told Farran magnanimously as she escorted the elderly woman, the most exhausting back-seat driver she had ever come across, to Miss Jessop's door.

'What time would you like me to call for you?' Farran enquired.

'I'll give you a ring when I'm ready,' she was informed, so that when Farran might have taken herself off for a walk, she had instead to return to the house so as to be within earshot for when the phone rang summoning her.

By Wednesday she had not seen again any trace of the sense of humour which she had thought Miss Irvine possessed. But by then Farran had gone through a period of adjustment, and, if still ticking the days off her calendar, she thought at least she could bear with her hostess's carping ways without erupting.

Although she was to find that she came close to answering back early that evening. They were sitting watching television—'watching' being the operative word, because Miss Irvine had a tendency to talk throughout any programme which Farran found interesting and made listening impossible—when Miss Irvine suddenly said, 'This programme's rubbish! Pass me the paper!'

Feeling astounded, because the paper, opened at the television page, was within an arm-stretch of Miss Irvine—while she would have to leave her chair and cross the floor to get it for her—Farran came close to commenting that she was sure a little exercise could do her nothing but good. Then all at once Nona Irvine smiled.

Suddenly, as Farran glimpsed a hint of something placatory in her hostess's look, she wondered if—as children test parents to see how far they can go—Miss Irvine had been trying something similar. Had she, Farran wondered, for the sake of some devilment, been trying to push her to the limits? Had she maybe read a touch of mutiny in her eyes just now, and decided it might be politic to smile?

Whatever was the case, in no time flat Miss Irvine was succeeding in making Farran thoroughly ashamed of herself and her mutinous thoughts when, with a small sigh, she requested, 'While you're on your feet, Farran, do you think you could ring Dr Richards' surgery? The arthritis in my shoulder is playing me up a little today— I think I'd better have a repeat of my last prescription.'

Farran was in a much chastened mood the following morning. She spent a lot of her time running around fetching and carrying for Miss Irvine, but when she was not doing that she would leave off midway through whatever chore she was doing to surreptitiously check on her.

Again and again she wondered how she could have let herself forget Nona Irvine's advanced years. True, there had been more in that good lady to resemble a dragon than a paragon—but she was being rather angelic this morning.

Farran was to have second thoughts on Miss Irvine's angelic disposition before the morning was over, though. Deciding to break off her chores and to go and have a cup of coffee with her, Farran loaded up a tray and carried it into the sitting-room. With Miss Irvine remaining quite amicable, elevenses had stretched to a quarter to twelve when she suddenly brought the subject round to Farran, and began asking her about her friends.

'Friends' to Farran immediately conjured up memories of Russell Ottley. She supposed it was a moot point as to whether they had ever been friends. But she had come close to having her fingers burned in that 'friendship' and was anxious to get the subject away from herself.

'How about you?' she turned the question back, and having met the three ladies she played bridge with, 'You seem to have a fair number of friends, Miss Irvine,' she smiled.

'Acquaintances!' that lady replied. 'All I have are acquaintances. I haven't got any true friends,' she sighed dramatically, and as Farran began to wish she had never turned the question back at her, Nona Irvine started to look quite downcast. Suddenly, though, a thought must have struck her, and she perked up. 'Except for Stallard, of course,' she stated. 'Now he's been a pillar of support to me—a very true friend.'

Farran, however, felt that, while she did not want to talk of Russell Ottley, neither did she want to talk of

Stallard Beauchamp, or hear Miss Irvine sing his praises, thank you very much. Which was why, in an attempt to hurriedly divert her, she found herself blurting out, 'You were very great friends with his mother too, I believe?' and was left staring at the change that came over Miss Irvine.

For all sign of amiability abruptly dropped away, and there was nothing but hate in her eyes as she retorted vehemently, 'That *woman* was *never* a friend of mine!'

'Oh, I'm—dreadfully sorry,' Farran said hastily. 'Stallard never said . . . I just thought . . .' Oh, grief, she thought as Nona Irvine glared at her with hostile eyes. To her great relief, however, just then the doorbell sounded. 'I'll go,' she said quickly, and, much shaken that anyone could hate another person as much as Nona Irvine appeared to hate Stallard's mother, she went to the door.

'Tad Richards—Dr Richards.' A brown-haired man of average height, and who seemed to be about thirty, fixed her with a blue-eyed look and introduced himself. 'Was it you who rang last night asking for a repeat prescription?'

'Yes,' answered Farran. 'I was told to call for it this afternoon.'

'I knew I was right when instinct told me to deliver the prescription in person,' he smiled, and with a glance down to her ringless left hand, 'Miss . . .'

'Farran Henderson,' she obliged, and told him, 'I'm Miss Irvine's new companion.'

'And a great improvement on the last one,' he replied with alacrity.

The fact that the doctor was not backward in coming forward did not pass Farran by. She was, however, more concerned to know if she had done any lasting harm to Miss Irvine by so unwittingly causing her upset than worried over the flirtatious doctor. 'Actually,' she told him, in a lowered tone, 'I wonder if you'd take a look at Miss Irvine if you've time.'

'She's not well?' he became all doctor to enquire.

'A remark I've just made has upset her,' Farran confessed.

'I shouldn't worry over one remark.' Tad Richards grinned as he stepped into the hall. 'Have you not yet seen the way they go for each other's throats when Miss Irvine and her chums play bridge?'

'Dr Richards has called with your prescription,' Farran told a sour-faced Miss Irvine as she led the way into the sitting-room.

'How's my favourite actress?' she was startled to hear him enquire of his patient. But as Farran collected up the used coffee things and took a glance in Nona Irvine's direction, she saw that Miss Irvine was smiling sweetly at the doctor rather than scowling sourly. Farran took the tray of china back to the kitchen.

She was still there, having washed up, and was making preparation for the light lunch they would have when Tad Richards came looking for her. 'Is she all right?' she asked him quickly.

'On top form, as usual,' he replied without hesitation.

'Thank goodness!' Farran said with relief, and saw Tad Richards' grin appear again.

'Don't take it so to heart,' he bade her lightly. 'Life wouldn't be life for Nona Irvine if something didn't occasionally happen to make her adrenalin flow.'

'It wouldn't?' she questioned, and, with something of a shock, she heard Tad Richards explain the 'How's my favourite actress?' remark with which he had greeted Miss Irvine.

'You knew she was on the stage at one time?' he enquired, and when Farran wordlessly shook her head he went on to tell her how, although Nona Irving had never made it to the top, she had been much in demand as a bit-part actress prior to her retirement. Then, having acquainted her with what most people in Low Monkton knew, apparently, Tad Richards went on to comment, 'Since it's easy to see that you're new to the area, it's clear that you'll be in need of a guide to the theatres and restaurants we can provide. Perhaps I can put myself forward as an...'

'In point of fact,' Farran cut him off, but finding that she had to smile none the less, 'I know the area fairly well.' She forbore to tell him of her knowledge of High Monkton and its surroundings through her many visits to Miss Newbold, but turned the subject back to the ex-actress. 'So I've no need to worry unduly over Miss Irvine's health?' she enquired.

With his hopes of a date dashed, Tad Richards smiled wryly, but answered her question. 'There's not much wrong that having her card-playing pals around won't cure,' he promised. 'Invite her chums to tea,' he suggested, 'and she'll soon forget any upset you may have inadvertently caused her.'

Farran went to work on his advice over lunch. Though since it was not up to her to invite Miss Irvine's 'chums' into her house, it called for the utmost tact. The fact that she had driven her to Mrs Jessop's home last Tuesday for a bridge game came in very useful.

'I was wondering whether, if it's your turn to have the game here next Tuesday, there's anything you'd like me to prepare in advance?' Farran suggested.

'Prepare?' Miss Irvine queried coldly.

'In the way of food?' Farran smiled, feigning ignorance as to whether she had taken tea at Miss Jessop's last week, but having not forgotten the relish with which Miss Irvine had tucked into her dinner on Tuesday evening.

'Food?' Nona Irvine, her voice still cold, questioned.

'Do you not do any entertaining?' Farran pressed on with a smile. 'Dinner parties or anything like that?' she added.

'How can I have a dinner party?' Miss Irvine added, 'Who would cook for me?'

'I would,' Farran replied promptly, and it was too late, as a thaw began on Nona Irvine's features, to wish she had thought about it a little first. Because, when Farran's mind had been on tea, it soon became clear that Miss Irvine had latched on to the idea of a dinner party—and, it transpired, not next Tuesday, but the following night!

'Are you sure it won't be too much for you?' was the only question she asked, and when she came back from a trip to the chemist to get her prescription made up she discovered that Miss Irvine had the dinner menu already worked out. Not only that, but she had already been on to Lydia Collier, Celia Ellams and Joan Jessop who, without exception, had accepted her invitation to dine.

As things turned out, Farran quite enjoyed the cooking involved. Miss Irvine helped too, in that, before she went to rest for the afternoon, she laid the table.

While the dinner went off very well, however, matters quickly deteriorated when—it going without saying that the four elderly ladies would play bridge after dinner—Joan Jessop discovered that she had left her bridge-playing glasses at home.

'It's too late to go back for them now!' she wailed, and did not look any happier when Nona Irvine gave her a withering look for her stupidity.

'There's nothing for it—Farran will have to play.'

'But I don't!' Farran tried to protest, with her mind on the mountain of washing-up in the kitchen.

What followed was for Farran, who knew next to nothing of card games, little short of two and a half hours of near-hell. Countless were the times she had to bite her tongue when Miss Irvine bullied her for some mistake. Though, from the sharp words which Lydia Collier and Celia Ellams exchanged from time to time, Farran fast formed the view that you didn't have to be naturally cantankerous to play bridge—but it helped.

'Can I get you a coffee or something, Mrs Jessop?' she asked when, in the dummy position, she had no part to play in the game, and observed Mrs Jessop unhappily looking on.

'Thank you, no,' Joan Jessop replied. 'It will only keep me awake tonight.' Farran was about to turn back to the table when, word clearly having been passed around about her family link with Miss Newbold, 'You'll be getting over Miss Newbold's death now, I imagine,' Mrs Jessop ventured, and, with an inquisitive look in her eyes, 'Dear Hetty, if she wasn't always changing her will towards the end, she was always adding something to it. I suppose,' she added, smiling falsely, 'that things were left the way they were supposed to be left?'

'I'm sure they were,' Farran smiled, feeling the evening could not deteriorate any further.

'Shush!' Nona Irvine quietened them in a boom of a voice, adding, 'Now look what you've made me do— I've roughed my own trick!'

Farran went to bed that night wondering how a dinner party that had started out so well could have deteriorated into such a disharmonious party that had ended in such disagreement, with failures at the card table still being dissected as the guests went out through the front door.

She got up late on Saturday morning—and knew she had been wrong to go to bed with the washing-up still piled up, and the kitchen looking as though a bomb had hit it. In truth, however, she had felt worn to a frazzle when the game had finished last night and had felt not the slightest guilt at ignoring the mess that awaited her in the kitchen.

After her bath, Farran donned a pair of good quality trousers and a sweater, then went quickly down the stairs to discover that not only was the kitchen a tip, but that somehow the four elderly ladies—and herself—had managed to make the sitting-room a disaster area too.

Miss Irvine, when she eventually arrived downstairs, was not in a very good mood. 'I'll just go and get your breakfast,' Farran told her, and sped away to try and find some space in the kitchen before Nona Irvine could make her habitual reminder about not requiring lumps in her porridge.

Forgoing breakfast herself, Farran decided to go and make the sitting-room comfortable for Miss Irvine to relax in after breakfast. A scalded cat had nothing on her as she raced around putting cards and the card table away, and returning chairs to their proper places. She opted for the carpet sweeper rather than the vacuum cleaner, and half an hour later the room resembled the way it should look, when Nona Irvine sailed majestically in.

'You'll never make a bridge player!' she sniffed in passing.

Since it seemed to her that all bridge players ever did was to constantly row about each other's bad play, Farran was not unhappy about that, and went to clear away in the breakfast-room.

Deciding that Miss Irvine would keep herself occupied with reading the paper and attempting the crossword for the next hour, she went into the kitchen, surveyed the mess, and thought—oh, hell! What was she doing here?

Knowing full well what she was doing there, Farran was nevertheless caught by a stray moment of rebellion, and could not see why she should not have herself a cup of coffee before she got stuck into saucepans, plates, side plates and every other piece of fine china with which Miss Irvine had decorated the table.

She had just immersed her hands in hot sudsy water after her coffee, however, when suddenly the front door bell pealed. Drying her hands as she went, she went to answer it.

'I knew I shouldn't have got up this morning,' she said grumpily, pulling back the door to find Stallard Beauchamp looking down his straight arrogant nose at her. *He* was all she needed! 'Miss Irvine's in the sitting-room,' she told him tartly, and leaving him to close the front door after him, she retraced her steps to the kitchen.

To her surprise, though, not to say annoyance, before she could again attempt to make a start on the washing-up she saw that he had not gone on down the hall to the sitting-room, but had followed her into the kitchen.

His expression, she saw, as his eyes went round the room to where every available surface appeared to have some piece of soiled china on it, mirrored disbelief.

'Ye gods!' he exclaimed, his eyes settling on the mountain of dirty dishes on the draining board. 'By the look of it you haven't washed up for a week!'

Farran had not been in her best mood before she had opened the door to him. She could not say that her mood had improved to have him still looking down his nose—and accusatory with it.

'Without help,' she snapped, 'the impossible takes a little longer!'

'Confound it, woman,' Stallard roared, 'Nona's in her eightieth year!'

Farran had not meant Miss Irvine but Mrs Lunn, the cleaning lady whom Miss Irvine had dismissed but who, had things been different, might have come in to give her a hand if asked. But having been misunderstood, she was in no mood to explain. It had been a week since she had seen Stallard Beauchamp. But having seen him, in no time she was once again experiencing that familiar feeling of wanting to physically set about him.

Suddenly Farran found she still held the towel on which she had dried her hands. Without thinking further, she aimed it furiously straight at him.

'Since you're so house-proud,' she exploded as she made for the kitchen door, '*you* do it!'

'This is how you intend to earn your inheritance, is it?' he growled before she could go through the door.

'Get lost!' Farran spat, and as she charged from the kitchen, she cared not a scrap about the inheritance or anything else.

CHAPTER FIVE

GRADUALLY Farran began to cool down. She had rushed up to her room, too furious with Stallard Beauchamp to care a whistle about the inheritance. But, as the heat of anger departed, she reluctantly realised that she just could not afford to go around telling the awful man to get lost, because there was not only herself to consider.

Kick against that fact though she might, she was still forced to accept that for Georgia's sake, and for Uncle Henry's, her temper and pride had to be sacrificed.

Farran was still not feeling very affable towards Stallard Beauchamp, however, when she left her room and went unenthusiastically down the stairs. She could hear the murmur of voices as she passed the sitting-room door, and hoped he would make this visit as short if not shorter than his last. With the kitchen such a tip it could take couple of hours to clear up—if luck was on her side he might leave without her having to see him again.

Going into the kitchen, she emptied the cooling sudsy water away and ran some more hot. She was just about to get started on the mountain of washing-up again, though, when the door opened and the male footfall behind her told her that today was not her lucky day.

She decided to ignore him and, tackling some saucers first, had just lifted one out of the water when she discovered that Stallard was not a man one could ignore. Particularly she could not ignore him when his way of making his presence felt was to cause her to turn and look at him—not believing her ears.

For 'I owe you an apology,' she distinctly heard him say.

'You're apologising!' she exclaimed, her pride not so buried that she could not find a little sarcasm to help her exclamation.

'I was in the wrong,' he owned, with the air of a man who hoped he was always big enough to apologise when at fault.

'That must be a first!' she found more sarcasm to toss another cold exclamation at him.

'Are you always so unforgiving?' he grunted.

'You could try grovelling on bended knee,' Farran suggested, but, as she saw a hint of movement at the corner of his mouth, as if she had just amused him and he was trying hard to suppress that amusement, she suddenly found she was feeling less aggressive towards him than she had done. 'What brought this on?' she questioned as she turned back to the sink and recommenced washing-up. His answer had her looking up at him in astonishment.

'I've just been hearing Nona singing your praises.' he told her as he came to stand by her side at the sink.

'Nona?' she gasped. 'The same Miss Irvine who's . . .' she broke off. If Miss Irvine had been singing her praises, it hardly seemed cricket to tell him what a thoroughly bad-tempered old battleaxe that lady had been to her for most of the week.

'The same,' Stallard replied, and went on, 'Nona, I'm afraid, is occasionally a little forgetful, and forgot last week, when I asked her if she had any problems, that she had dismissed her domestic help.'

'It—er—must be difficult to remember everything,' murmured Farran, having only last night seen Miss Irvine's fantastic memory in evidence when, in the post-mortem that followed every hand, she was able to remember every card and every sequence in which each of the fifty-two cards had been played. To her mind Miss Irvine had a conveniently forgetful memory when it came to disclosing how—basically because of her nagging— two people had departed the household within days of each other.

'Nona tells me that as well as being her companion, you did all the cleaning last week and also cooked a superb dinner for her and her guests last evening.'

'I shouldn't like you to think I was taking your money under false pretences,' murmured Farran, having not yet banked the cheque he had given her, and uncertain that she would anyhow.

'I wouldn't think there's much fear of that,' he drawled. 'Not while you're doing the work of three people.'

Really, Farran thought, her acid dissolving completely, when he chose to put himself out, he was actually quite charming. 'Would you like coffee?' she found herself asking—and could not understand the thundering in her ribs when he smiled, reached for the drying-up cloth, and said easily,

'When we've dealt with this lot.'

Farran turned back to the washing-up. 'I did intend to do it last night,' she found herself excusing, 'only...'

'Only Mrs Jessop forgot her bridge specs and you were roped in to play.' Farran scrubbed at more dishes. By the sound of it Miss Irvine had held back nothing! 'I've told Nona that she must advertise for another cleaner. Perhaps you'll remind her if she forgets,' Stallard added pleasantly.

'You—er—shouldn't be doing this,' Farran told him a minute or so later.

'I shouldn't?'

'You should be keeping Miss Irvine company,' she explained. 'It's not fair on her if you spend half of your visit in the kitchen.'

'Oh, I don't intend to do that,' he replied.

'You don't?' she queried.

'I hope not,' he said, looking steadily at her as he added, 'An hour or so out of the weekend doesn't constitute half, does it?'

'You're staying the weekend?'

'If you've no objection,' he replied.

'Be my guest,' Farran replied, and laughed, enjoying it when he laughed, and discovered with some surprise that she did not mind too much at all that he would be under the same roof as her for longer than the couple of hours, at the most, which she had expected him to be there.

That was not the only occasion when Stallard helped with the washing-up. With the hour rapidly approaching noon by the time the kitchen was once more respectable, and they had all had coffee in the sitting-room, Farran set about finding something for lunch.

She decided to go to town on the evening meal, so lunch was a light meal of tinned soup, gammon and pineapple with a salad, with fresh fruit to follow. Lunchtime passed most pleasantly, with Miss Irvine either delighted to see Stallard, or on her best behaviour because he was there. Whatever, not one cross word fell from her lips. Though, because she liked to talk, many other words did, all of them agreeable.

'I'll give you a hand with the washing-up,' Stallard volunteered as he and Miss Irvine helped to clear the table afterwards.

'There's no need,' Farran told him, then realised that he was being tactful on account of knowing, as she did, that when she wasn't off somewhere for a game Nona Irvine liked a short nap after her midday meal. 'But if you insist,' Farran smiled, 'come this way.'

Running the taps into the sink, she could hardly believe that this charming, considerate and tactful man was

the same one who, not too long back, she had dubbed
as being a swine and a reptile.

'Where did you learn to cook?' he asked as he stood
beside her at the kitchen sink.

'Give gammon a grill and it has a tendency to cook
itself, and salad doesn't require much cooking,' she replied lightly.

'And last night's efforts?' he queried.

'Mrs Fenner, our housekeeper, let me into a few of
her culinary secrets in my teenage years,' she told him,
feeling complimented.

There was a moment's pause, then he asked, his tone
even, 'Did you do much cooking in Hong Kong?' and
any pleased feelings she had abruptly vanished.

'Some,' she answered briefly, not wanting to be reminded of Russell Ottley—not that she had ever cooked
him a meal—or to be reminded of Stallard's more usual
manner with her whenever Hong Kong was mentioned.

But neither her short tone nor her monosyllabic reply
were as off-putting to him as she had hoped. For it appeared he had another question lined up. 'Why,' he
began, '*did* you leave Hong Kong so hurriedly, Farran?'

For all of thirty seconds Farran was totally non-
plussed. Shooting him a startled glance, she saw that his
eyes were steady upon her, and she looked swiftly away
again. This was the first intimation she had had that he
might be on the way to changing his opinion that she
had dashed home with all speed to claim her inheritance! But she did not want him probing into her personal life.

'Who says I left Hong Kong in a hurry?' she answered
his question with a question of her own.

'You did,' he replied, not in the least put off.

'I *didn't*!' Farran said sharply, unable to remember
exactly what she had said, and hoping it was the same
with him.

'You implied it!' he countered, revealing that he was a man who missed very little, either said or implied. 'It was there in your statement of how you'd given up your job and flown home.'

Farran gave him an annoyed look, and had turned back to accelerate her dishwashing when she discovered that he did not give a damn how she looked when he was intent on getting the answers he wanted.

Though several degrees of frost had been added to his tone as he stated, 'It was because of some man, of course.'

Wondering when it was that she had ever thought of Stallard Beauchamp as not being a swine, she snapped, 'Why "of course"?'

'To my certain knowledge you have the ability to work hard,' he retorted—without making it sound like a compliment, for his voice was no warmer. 'If you can give a one-hundred-per-cent effort to a companion's job you've no liking for, I can't see you being dismissed for giving less to a secretarial job which you must have liked better.'

'Well, I would give my all here, wouldn't I?' she got in shortly to try and detract him from his intent. 'The rewards from this companion's job promise to...'

'Which,' he cut in deliberately, causing her more annoyance, 'leaves me to assume that you left Hong Kong in such a hurry because you were having an affair that...'

'I was *not* having an affair!' Farran erupted without thought, turning to glare furiously at him. 'I left because I did not *want* an affair!' she exploded, then halted, and could have groaned out loud at what he had goaded her into saying.

'It couldn't have been because you're frigid,' he commented coldly, his steely-eyed look on the passionate fury in her eyes.

Farran felt very much like marching out of the kitchen at that juncture. But she had stormed out of the kitchen away from him once before today, and she was suddenly visited by a streak of stubbornness that insisted that she stay and stand her ground. 'Why I left ... Why I ...' she faltered, and then, hating him again with a vengeance, she discovered that when she had been about to tell him that it was no business of his whatsoever, she found that what she was actually telling him was a hostile, 'To save you working it out, he was married.' A hint of sarcasm was thrown in too.

The frost that had been in his voice before was there again when he demanded harshly, 'You make a habit of having affairs with married men?'

'No!' rocketed from her in an angry denial. 'Haven't I just said that I left because I didn't want an ...'

'So what was so special about this one?' he growled.

'I fell in love with him,' snapped Farran, and as Stallard gave her a dark glowering look, 'That's what was so special about him,' she said defiantly.

'Naturally he wanted an affair with you,' he clipped.

'What he wanted,' she retorted, suddenly starting to feel sick inside, 'was some sordid kind of affair behind his wife's back!'

'You'd have preferred that his wife knew about it?' asked Stallard with stony sarcasm.

'I thought they were separating,' Farran had started to explain. Then she thought angrily, damn Stallard Beauchamp, who the blazes did he think he was, to put her through this? It was nothing to do with him what she did, or didn't do, for that matter. 'OK, so I was in the wrong,' she said aloofly, 'but I didn't realise ... I didn't ...' Suddenly she was as angry with herself as she was with Stallard, and terminated the conversation with the terse sentence, 'I wasn't in line for any casual affair—so I came home.'

In arctic silence they continued with the dishes. That Stallard had allowed her to terminate the conversation, Farran realised as one plate and then another was quickly washed, rinsed and then passed over to him, was only because he had got out of her everything he wanted to know.

Not that he believed her, she was sure of that, as she tackled the grill pan. She was convinced that he, having got her closest secrets out of her, had soon made up his mind to stick with his original belief, that the only reason she had raced back to England was because of the pickings to be had on the death of Miss Newbold.

Farran finished the washing-up and had the dishcloth in her hands ready to wipe a few surfaces as Stallard dried the last of the washing up and put the tea-towel down.

He looked as friendly towards her as she was feeling towards him when he said tersely, 'I'm taking Nona for a drive—are *you* coming?'

I'd cut my throat sooner, Farran thought. 'No, I'm not!' she answered sharply, and added, 'Even skivvies have some time off!'

It did not come as any great surprise that, pausing only to serve her a look of intense dislike, Stallard Beauchamp should go striding from the kitchen.

Perhaps her remark about 'skivvies' had made her sound as if she felt hard done by, Farran mused, as she wiped work surfaces and set about making the kitchen spick and span. But who in creation cared anyway? Certainly not her! Stallard Beauchamp could go and jump over a railway bridge—preferably when there was a train coming—as far as she was concerned.

She was just taking a last inspecting eye round, when the kitchen door opened. Determinedly she kept her back to it. Then, when she was positive it was Stallard come to make some acid comment, she was startled to hear the clear tones of Miss Irvine as she called her name.

'Farran,' she said, and as Farran spun round to see that Miss Irvine was wearing a topcoat and another of her outrageous hats, she went on, 'Stallard and I are just off out. I wonder, dear, could I ask you to make up a bed for him in the best spare room while we've gone?'

The 'dear' which Miss Irvine had called her, not to mention the polite way in which she had made her request, was not lost on Farran. My, we are on our best behaviour today! she thought. But, since *that brute* was staying overnight, and since—if she didn't make a bed up for him—the eighty-year-old Miss Irvine would no doubt tackle the job herself, Farran saw she could do no other than agree.

'Of course I will,' she smiled, wondering where, in deepest Dorset on a Saturday afternoon, one could purchase a bed of nails. 'Enjoy your outing,' she bade the elderly lady, and later she went upstairs to carry out her promise to Miss Irvine while at the same time she mutinied that Stallard Beauchamp was big enough to make his own bed.

Deciding that, even though she hated the swine like poison, she must not get small-minded, Farran, having checked that the room he would use was neat, tidy and dusted, returned to the kitchen to make a batch of scones.

Enjoying this short time on her own, she left the scones cooling on a rack once they were done, and felt suddenly out of sorts. Wondering if perhaps all she needed was to speak to someone who cared for her, she went to the phone. Realising the uselessness of ringing home, since Mrs Fenner always went to see her sister on a Saturday afternoon and Uncle Henry, having declined to have a phone in his workshop, would not hear the phone anyway, Farran chanced Georgia not being too busy to speak to her, and rang her at the salon.

'Everything all right?' Georgia asked quickly when she eventually came to the phone.

'Fine!' Farran told her, injecting a note of cheerfulness into her voice. 'How's everything with you?'

'Couldn't be better!' Georgia trilled, sounding so happy that Farran could not help feeling glad that she had, by virtue of the fact of agreeing to Stallard Beauchamp's terms, taken some of the pressure off her dear stepsister. 'I'm being paged,' Georgia said quickly. 'I must go. Give me your phone number,' she added hurriedly, 'and I'll give you a ring when I've got time for a longer chat.'

Farran gave her Miss Irvine's telephone number, but although she came away from the phone feeling good about Georgia, her feeling of being out of sorts was soon back. She decided, in the absence of having anything better to do, to go upstairs and have a wash and change.

She was on her way downstairs, however, when Miss Irvine came through the front door, followed by Stallard Beauchamp. She saw his eyes flick over her slender shape in her pure wool two-piece of houndstooth check, but from what she could tell from his taciturn expression he was in no pleasanter a humour than the last time she had seen him.

'You've been baking,' Miss Irvine observed as she sniffed the air.

'Just a few scones,' murmured Farran as she joined them in the hall. 'Did you enjoy the drive?'

'Stallard is such a good driver,' Miss Irvine replied, and as she divested herself of her hat and held it out for Farran to hold while she unbuttoned her coat, she went chattering on about every inconsequential incident of the drive.

'You'll be in need of a cup of tea, I expect,' Farran smiled, and while Miss Irvine and Stallard Beauchamp went into the sitting-room, a hugely delighted Farran went and stowed Miss Irvine's coat and hat away. By the sound of it, and the grim look on Stallard's face seemed to confirm it, Miss Irvine had been at her back-seat-driving worst for the entire outing!

Having a hard time not to burst out laughing as she visualised Miss Irvine insisting to Stallard, as she had to her last Tuesday, that it was quite in order for them to drive the wrong way down a one-way street, Farran returned to the kitchen to set the kettle to boil.

Wishing she had been a fly on the steering wheel, she felt fairly positive that Miss Irvine would have chattered away throughout the whole of the drive. If her own experience was anything to go by, she would at some point have told him, too, that they must turn left just as, with another car on their bumper, they were passing the left turn.

Farran got out delicate cups and saucers, remembering how, on the one and only time she had taken the car out Miss Irvine, in her fine voice, had suddenly exclaimed in anguish, 'Oh, my heart!' and as Farran instinctively put her foot down and prepared to race to the nearest hospital, 'Just look what the new owners have done to Mabel Armstrong's front lawn!' she had added.

Farran had never enquired who Mabel Armstrong was, and they had been too far past that lady's ex-house for her to see—traffic permitting her to take her eyes off the road—what the new owners had done to the lawn. Though, as she set the sugar bowl and milk jug on a tray, Farran felt she could be sure that since Miss Irvine seemed to believe that one had no need to watch the road but could view the scenery or turn one's head to observe anything she happened to notice, it was a fair bet that Stallard had been suddenly told to 'Look over there!' or asked, 'Well, what do you think of that!'

With her thoughts happy ones, at that moment Farran came close to liking Miss Irvine. She was about to start slicing and buttering scones, however, when the kitchen door opened and Stallard Beauchamp walked in.

'Nona wants her glasses!' he said curtly.

Calmly Farran cut a scone in half. 'She does some-times,' she replied, and heard him take a long-suffering breath.

'Have you seen them?' he demanded impatiently.

Biting down a snappy 'Often!' Farran tossed him and his irritated expression a cool glance. At a guess Miss Irvine had checked her handbag without success. 'Try her coat pocket—it's hanging up in the cloakroom,' she told him evenly, thinking Miss Irvine must have taken her half-moon glasses off and slipped them into her coat pocket before she had gone out.

Thank you, most kind, Farran thought tartly as Stallard left the kitchen en route for the cloakroom. She had done little more than neatly place the buttered scones on a plate, though, than he was back again.

'Nona,' he clipped, 'wants her cardigan.' Keeping her face deadpan, Farran looked at him with wide brown innocent eyes. 'She can't remember where she left it,' Stallard added, and to her mind he seemed to be having difficulty in keeping his temper in check.

Having spent a week of fetching and carrying for Miss Irvine, and fast forming the view that this was the longest amount of time he had spent in the ex-actress's company, so he had no idea of how demanding she could be on occasion, a slow, sweet smile broke on Farran's features.

'Her cardigan's in her bedroom. I hung it up in her wardrobe when I turned the central heating up just before you came back in,' she told him nicely.

She had made a pot of tea and had added that, with three plates, to the tea tray when, looking as though he was about to breathe fire down his nostrils at any moment, Stallard once more came into the kitchen.

'Her knitting's down by the side of her usual chair,' Farran told him before he could open his mouth.

'She doesn't want tea,' he gritted through clenched teeth as, ignoring what she had said, he delivered the message he had been sent to deliver, 'she wants milk.'

With that he went to turn about. But Farran was only human. 'Confound it, man,' she mocked, 'she *is* in her eightieth year, you know.' Oh, grief, she thought, and as Stallard took a threatening step forward she was certain that, just as she had often felt like hitting him, he was now not only reciprocating those feelings but was about to do something fairly violent about them.

To her tremendous relief, however, all he did, as she took a hasty step backwards, was to take up the heavily laden tray which he espied standing on the kitchen table.

'You bring her milk!' he ordered, and, carrying the tray, he left her staring after him.

He was something of a contradiction, Farran mused as she found a glass and poured some milk into it. For, when it was certain that he was not only fed up to the back teeth but angry as well, all the same, when he had spotted the laden tea tray, his innate sense of courtesy had dictated that he should carry it through to the sitting-room for her.

Miss Irvine was dispensing tea when Farran joined her and Stallard in the sitting-room. She saw that his courtesy was still holding up as he accepted a cup of tea and a plate with a scone on it. Then, clearly of the view that since she was there he could take a rest from his fetching and carrying, he excused himself and hid behind the daily newspaper. Farran smiled. She well knew that if Miss Irvine felt like talking then the barricade of a newspaper would be insufficient to stop her flow—and so it proved.

'These scones are delicious, Farran,' she complimented her. 'Aren't they, Stallard?' she addressed his newspaper.

Farran thought she heard him draw another exasperated breath, and had adopted her 'innocent' expression when she saw him slowly lower his paper. She saw him glance at Miss Irvine, and then at her, but felt more that he intended to offend than second Miss Irvine's opinion of her scones when he replied, 'They're—quite—unbelievable,' and raised his paper in front of him.

Pig! thought Farran, and came nearer still to liking Miss Irvine when she cheerfully addressed him once more through the back of his newspaper. In all, Miss Irvine had him lowering his paper three times before, as always unfailingly polite and courteous in his replies to her, he gave up all attempts to read it.

At which point Miss Irvine found something she wanted to discuss with Farran. 'Can you find a dropped stitch for me?' she asked, putting her milk glass down on the side table Stallard had pulled up for her. 'I know I had seventy-five stitches to start with,' she said, reaching down to the side of her chair and putting her knitting bag on her lap, 'but when I counted them earlier, there were only seventy-four.'

Taking hold of the piece of knitting which Miss Irvine extracted from her bag, Farran was glad to see that her ambitions did not go beyond stocking-stitch.

Studying the knitting for a minute or so, she said, 'Here it is!' and, having found the dropped stitch about twelve inches from the top, she patiently worked the stitch back up from row to row. 'That's it,' she said, handing the work back to Miss Irvine. Then, turning to collect the tea tray, she caught Stallard's eyes on her, and realised he must have been watching her for some time.

Why just the mere fact of him watching her should make her heart suddenly skip a beat, Farran had no idea. Though she was sure it was not because his expression had lost its aggression and that he looked as if he might smile at her.

Whether he did smile at her or not, though, Farran did not discover. For just then the phone rang, and her attention went from him to where the phone was—near Miss Irvine's hand.

Sure that the phone call was not for her, Farran quietly stacked used china and the empty milk glass on the tray as Miss Irvine picked up the phone and said, 'Hello.' Farran was making certain that the tray was safe to carry when, every bit as if she was acting the role of a parlourmaid, she heard Miss Irvine ask pleasantly, 'Who shall I say is calling?'

At that point Farran knew without question that Miss Irvine *did* have a sense of humour—albeit she only used it on a Saturday. Though when she was about to head for the kitchen with the tray, and thereby reduce the number of eavesdroppers to Stallard's call by one, she was suddenly made aware that she was mistaken in thinking the call must be for him.

'There's a Mr Andrew Watson on the line for you, Farran,' Miss Irvine told her affably, and held the phone out to her.

Farran was still getting over the fact that her one-time good friend Andrew Watson, with whom she had once attended every sporting function, was on the line. Andrew had moved away from Banford some years ago, yet, incredibly, he had somehow found her.

'Andrew?' she queried down the mouthpiece, and was delighted to hear her old friend again.

'What the deuce are you doing down in Dorset when this is my first day back in Banford?' a voice she remembered with affection asked.

'You're in Banford...' she began to query.

'I'm staying with my folks, but only until I find myself another travelling job,' he told her. And while it was registering that Andrew must have given up his old job, he was explaining that finding her had not been so incredibly difficult. 'I called round at your house, but your stepfather didn't seem to have much idea where you were, so he told me to go and ask Georgia.'

'Ah!' Farran saw it all.

'I knew I'd go through fire and water for you, Farran, but don't ever ask me to go into a ladies' beauty salon again!' he said to make her laugh.

'I won't, I promise,' she chuckled, and Andrew got to the point of his call.

'Georgia said something about you working at a live-in job, but I wondered if we could meet up next week on your day off?'

'I'd love to!' Farran said warmly, then recollected that she had no set 'off' time. She looked at Miss Irvine, intending to ask her if she could do without her for a few hours one day next week, when, flicking a glance at Stallard, she saw that he was watching her with a look that was little short of murderous! Shaken rigid, she swiftly took her eyes from him. 'I'm—er...' she began, and discovered that she had to search hard to pick up the thread of her conversation. 'Can you give me a ring next week?' she found herself suggesting.

'Nothing simpler,' he replied, and while she was still trying to decipher what Stallard Beauchamp's murderous look had been all about, Andrew, after chatting a few minutes longer, rang off.

Farran was still feeling shaken when, deciding to ignore Stallard Beauchamp, she recalled that she had been about to take the tea tray out to the kitchen. She was forestalled as she picked it up, though, for Stallard had left his chair, and in a few strides was taking the tray from her.

'Allow me,' he said civilly, and while she sensed that he wanted a not very pleasant word with her in private—

and for that reason she almost returned to her chair and let him cool his heels in the kitchen—some part of her that insisted, well, I'm not afraid of him, for goodness' sake, made her follow him from the sitting-room.

'Thanks,' she said as she entered the kitchen.

'Is Watson your married lover from Hong Kong?' Stallard Beauchamp fired at her without preamble.

'No, he's not!' she erupted, incensed on the instant by his outrageous nerve. 'Russell Ottley, as far as I know, is still in Hong Kong—and he was never my l...'

'Has this Watson been here to see you?' she was cut off before she could finish.

'No!' she snapped.

'What about other men?' he hurled at her. 'Might I remind you, you *are* here to do a job of work.'

The unfairness of it! 'My stars!' Farran exploded. 'I've been on pretty well non-stop since I first walked through the front door! As for other men,' she blazed on, astonished by his question because it was only that day that she had told him of her love for Russell, 'I've lived the life of a nun since I got here!'

'That won't hurt you for a change!' he snarled, and, frustrating Farran totally when she felt that any second now she was going to have the satisfaction of hitting him, he strode out of the kitchen.

Farran found a few more unpleasant names to add to the few she had specially reserved for him as, with more temper than care, she washed the cups, saucers and plates they had used. Fortunately, however, none of the delicate china came to grief.

After about half an hour spent in the kitchen, she felt her temper had come sufficiently off the boil for her to return to the sitting-room to see if there was anything in particular that Miss Irvine would like for dinner. To her joy, however, it seemed that Stallard was on the point of departing.

'Don't get up, Nona,' he was saying as she went in, 'I'll see myself out.'

'Stallard's leaving!' Nona Irvine looked across to Farran to bemoan as she saw her. 'He's just remembered something he has to return to London to do.'

Believing that in the face of Miss Irvine's distress it would be impolite of her to turn cartwheels at this news, Farran restrained herself. 'Oh dear,' she murmured, and, transferring her gaze to look into a pair of cold grey eyes that looked straight back at her, 'How sad,' she smiled sweetly.

From the sudden jut of his jaw she knew for a fact that he was perfectly well aware that she personally could not wait for him to be gone. Though as she saw the glitter of ice in the steady look he gave her, she had an awful feeling that for the simple pleasure of wiping the smile from her face, he was on the verge of changing his mind about the urgency of his return to London.

He did not change his mind, however. But long after he had gone, Farran was still wondering—why he had in fact gone at all. His excuse of having forgotten to do something in London was plainly that—an excuse. So what had made him change his mind about staying? She doubted, for all Miss Irvine had been a shade wearing that day, that she had so weakened his stamina that he had chosen to opt out.

It did not take Farran long after that to work out that she and she alone must be the culprit. For all her previous joy, though, it gave her something of a jolt, and a not very pleasant feeling inside. It was all very well for her to hate Stallard Beauchamp, but to know that he disliked her so much that a few hours spent in the same house as her were all that he could take was something which Farran found most disquieting.

CHAPTER SIX

SUNDAY dawned, a cold, chill day. It matched Farran's mood. She sighed as she got out of bed. Life was bleak— to match the weather. She was in the bathroom running her bath when the most absurd thought suddenly struck her. Could it be that she was feeling down because, with Stallard having returned to London, she had not the stimulus of crossing swords with him to look forward to?

Scorning any odd notion that she could possibly be wishing Stallard Beauchamp had not returned to London yesterday, Farran got busy with her ablutions. Perhaps living with Miss Irvine was having an unbalancing effect on her, she thought with a touch of humour.

To cheer her, Georgia rang just after breakfast to apologise for not having time to spare for a chat the day before.

'I didn't really expect you to have,' Farran smiled. 'I just rang to say hello. Things going smoothly with the alterations next door?'

'You're joking!' laughed Georgia. 'If it wasn't for my dear architect, I'd be off my head by now!'

'You did say you'd have to work closely with him over the alterations to the greengrocer's shop,' Farran recalled.

'He's—er—um—taking a special interest in what I'm doing,' Georgia told her, but she sounded so hesitant, and so unlike the confident stepsister Farran knew, that, with a start, she realised there was something more here— on Georgia's side, anyway—than a mere client-and-architect relationship.

'You're—still seeing him socially?' she asked, recalling that Georgia had once, to her knowledge, dined with him and, if she remembered correctly, had seemed quite smitten by the man—what was his name?—Idris Vaughan, that was it.

'Ye-es,' Georgia replied evasively. Previously she had talked openly about her men friends, but now she clearly wanted to leave it at that, so Farran just knew that her stepsister was either in love or on the brink of falling in love. 'Talking of social life, what do you do for laughs down there?' Georgia took the spotlight off herself.

'I attempted to play bridge on Friday,' Farran allowed herself to be sidetracked as she remembered how her attempt at the game had been more horrendous than amusing, while at the same time she hoped with all her heart that Georgia's love would have a happy outcome. 'And Andrew Watson rang yesterday.'

'He came into the salon. Was it all right to give him your number?'

'Fine,' Farran replied.

'And you're really getting on OK?'

'Of course,' Farran answered.

'The old dear's not as bad as you thought, then?'

'I'm getting quite to like her,' Farran replied, and later lived to rethink that remark. For no sooner had she and Georgia said goodbye than Miss Irvine came from the kitchen and complained long and hard about how she had left her with all the breakfast clearing up to do.

From then, right up until Tuesday, it seemed that Farran could do nothing right for her. There was no let-up from her on Tuesday afternoon either, she discovered, for it was Miss Irvine's turn to hostess the regular Tuesday afternoon bridge session, and even when she was playing cards Miss Irvine was not distracted from crotchety comment.

Much to Farran's relief, Miss Irvine decided she would have an early night that night. Even so, it was half-past ten before Farran escorted her, her drinking water, handbag and various impedimenta collected through the day up the stairs.

Think of Georgia and Uncle Henry, Farran told herself when, having run down the stairs again for Miss Irvine's book which she, according to accusation, had forgotten, and back up, she again returned down the stairs—this time to secure the house for the night.

Checking that the front door was locked and bolted, Farran went to check on the rear door, reminding herself that it was for only three months. The thought of spending many more days like the last three, however, was not a cheering thought, and she went hastily into the sitting-room to make sure all electrical switches were off and to try and think of pleasanter matters. Then the phone rang.

It was then that she remembered that Andrew Watson had been going to ring this week. She answered it, realising that although she had meant to ask Miss Irvine about having some time off, she had been in such a cantankerous mood she had not yet asked her.

'Hello,' she said, and felt that most peculiar fluttering sensation in her heart region again, when she recognised that it was not Andrew on the line, but Stallard Beauchamp.

'How—is everything!' he questioned her tersely.

'How would you expect everything to be?' snapped Farran, not needing his grouchy phone call on top of everything else.

'How are things with you and Nona?' he coldly rephrased his question.

'You wouldn't consider putting her in a nursing home, would you?' she retorted hopefully.

There was a moment or two's pause, then his tone suddenly changed to be more sympathetic than harsh, sounding as if he understood how difficult Nona Irvine could be when she made her mind up to it. 'That bad?' he enquired.

Immediately Farran felt ashamed. 'Not really,' she replied, all snappiness gone from her voice. 'Did you want to speak to her?' she enquired.

'Not really,' Stallard bounced her own two words back at her and, to her surprise, he rang off.

Left holding the phone, Farran began thinking that, because it was him, Miss Irvine would not have minded getting out of bed and coming to the phone. Then suddenly she realised that Stallard had not rung especially to speak to the near-octogenarian.

All at once a smile came to her face, because if he had not rung to speak to Miss Irvine then he had rung especially to speak to her—hadn't he? Which, even though his enquiry had been more about the two of them than her personally, had to mean that he did not dislike her as much as she had supposed—didn't it? The smile was still on Farran's mouth as she switched off the light and left the room.

Quite how things began to improve the next day, she was uncertain. All she knew was that winter did not seem so bleak when she opened her eyes the next morning, and that Miss Irvine, when she joined her downstairs, seemed to have wakened in a better humour than of late.

In fact, in such an improved humour was Miss Irvine that as they cleared away the breakfast things, Farran found herself referring to Andrew's telephone call last Saturday quite easily.

'He's your boyfriend?' Miss Irvine enquired.

'Not in the accepted sense of the word,' Farran replied. 'We were at school together and because we lived nearer to each other than any of the rest, we just sort of palled up. He's not working at the moment, so any day would be convenient for him to come to Low Monkton, I should imagine,' she said, having already mentioned how Andrew had said he would like to see her.

'And you would like to see him?' Miss Irvine asked cordially.

'I wouldn't mind,' Farran smiled—and could hardly credit her hearing at Miss Irvine's next remark.

'Why not invite him to lunch?' she suggested graciously.

'I . . .' gasped Farran, certain in her mind that Andrew had not envisaged sharing lunch with her and the eighty-year-old Miss Irvine when he had said he would like to meet up. But with Miss Irvine being so pleasant today, she had no intention of provoking a return to the Miss Irvine she better knew. Quickly Farran gathered her scattered senses. 'You wouldn't mind?' she queried.

'Not at all. I love company,' Miss Irvine smiled. Farran was still getting over the smile, the remark, when Miss Irvine asked, 'Did your friend Andrew telephone last evening? I thought I heard the phone just after I went to bed.'

'You did,' Farran agreed. 'But it wasn't Andrew, it was Stallard. He . . .'

'Stallard?' Miss Irvine interrupted, but, although she was clearly regretful that she had missed speaking with him, her tone was not cross when she said, 'You should have called me, I'd have put on a dressing-gown and come down.'

'I'm sorry.' Farran felt it wouldn't hurt to apologise.

'Never mind,' Nona Irvine said genially. 'Did he leave any message?'

'He didn't stay talking long—he just wanted to know how you were,' Farran told her, a white lie permissible, she thought, in the circumstance of Stallard asking how things were with her and Miss Irvine.

This time she was not surprised when Miss Irvine smiled. Nor, since she had already gleaned that Stallard was one of life's 'special' people to the elderly lady, was she surprised to hear her say, 'He's such a dear man!' What did surprise her, however, was that she should gently tack on, 'So like his very dear father.'

Feeling shaken to hear the gentle, almost reverent way in which she had spoken of Stallard's father, Farran contrasted the way there had been hate in Miss Irvine's eyes when she had spoken of Stallard's mother. 'That *woman* was *never* a friend of mine,' she recalled her stoutly maintaining.

'You're—friends with Stallard's father?' Farran felt on safer ground in asking. She was again shaken by Miss Irvine's reply.

'Murdoch Beauchamp is dead,' she sighed, but added, 'He and I were more than friends,' and from the tender way she said his name Farran just knew that Nona Irvine had been in love with Stallard's father.

Before Farran had fully grasped that Miss Irvine might, from her remark of being more than friends with Murdoch Beauchamp, have been implying that they had been lovers, the telephone rang. Miss Irvine went to answer it.

'It's for you,' she told Farran, and as she handed over the phone, she said in a stage whisper, 'It's your friend Andrew. Ask him to lunch.'

'I have the whole of tomorrow at your disposal,' Andrew told Farran. 'Any good?'

'Come to lunch,' she obliged dutifully, and came away from the phone to tell her waiting hostess, 'He's coming tomorrow, Miss Irvine. Is that all right?'

'That settles it,' Miss Irvine declared. 'We'll go shopping.' She was on her way to put on her hat and coat when she paused. 'By the way,' she added, 'please call me Nona—"Miss Irvine" makes me feel old!'

It was good to see Andrew again. He was a rather nice kind of person, and with his natural 'niceness' and with Miss Irvine staying in the same good humour she had been in the previous day, the extended lunch passed off exceedingly well.

'You must come and visit us again, Andrew,' Nona Irvine told him with gracious charm as she and Farran waved him off.

'Thank you, I'd like to,' he replied, and cheerfully roared down the drive in his car.

That Nona Irvine had not turned into a complete lamb overnight was evinced again on Friday morning when, as on Wednesday, Farran took her out in the car. It had been in her mind to take her for a nice long drive around the crisp countryside, but half an hour of Nona back-seat driving from the front passenger seat was enough to have Farran turn the car around and head for home. That outing lasted an hour, and her respect for Stallard went up a hundredfold. He had taken Nona out for a drive last Saturday—they had been out for going on *two* hours!

Back at the house, Farran felt in the need of something stronger than coffee to soothe her jangled nerves, but she made coffee for her and Nona, and had just taken it into the sitting-room when someone rang the doorbell.

'No peace for the wicked,' Nona said drily, and as Farran went to answer the door she had to wonder if Nona's sense of humour was showing again. Did she in fact know how she had wrecked any peace she might have found in this last hour?

Whatever the fact of the matter, Farran could not restrain a smile at Nona's droll sense of humour. A smile was still on her lips when she opened the door to find Dr Richards standing there.

'Now that's a nice welcome!' he greeted her.

'Come in,' she bade him, and, thinking this must be one of his routine visits, told him, 'Miss Irvine's in the sitting-room.'

'Who says I've come to see Miss Irvine?' he grinned impudently.

'I'm not your patient, Dr Richards.' Farran attempted to sound prim.

'All to the good, *Farran*,' he replied promptly, 'otherwise I'd have to think twice about taking you out to dinner tonight.'

Giving him a look for his sauce, Farran—whether he liked it or not—headed for the sitting-room, opened the door, and called, 'Here's Dr Richards!'

'You weren't so attentive to me before Farran came here.' Nona saw straight through him the moment he followed Farran into the sitting-room.

'How can you say that?' he laughed, but he seemed the best of friends with Nona, who, laughing too, asked him if he wanted a cup of coffee.

When later Farran saw Tad Richards out, she had declined to go out to dinner with him, but had softened what he would have her believe was a mortifying blow by agreeing to call him Tad.

'If I were a corny kind of guy, I'd say something like "It's a good job I'm a doctor with plenty of patients",' he quipped.

'Goodbye, Tad,' Farran bade him.

The rest of that day passed uneventfully with Nona going up to bed at around ten-thirty, and with Farran going up the stairs with her carrying the various trivia which Nona had gathered around her during the day. Then, as was now routine, Farran returned downstairs to secure the house for the night.

When she too finally went back up the stairs, she owned to feeling in a tense sort of mood. Something floating between feeling a little out of sorts and being a shade keyed up was the best way she felt to describe it, as she climbed into bed.

When she awakened on Saturday, however, Farran was fairly astounded to discover that, while the tense mood of last night still lingered in the background, she was better able to put a finger on it that morning. For, shatteringly, she realised she was in a state of suspense—from hoping Stallard Beauchamp would pay them a visit that day!

Nothing if not honest, Farran went through the ritual of bathing and dressing, trying to dissect why it should bother her whether he paid them a visit at Low Monkton that day or not.

After last Saturday's visit, and the way they exchanged verbal acid, she would have thought she'd be cheering from the rooftops if she never saw him again. Yet…was it perhaps that, with Nona being such a better-natured person these last few days, she was missing the cut and thrust of verbal battle?

A few minutes later, having recalled that she had never gone into verbal battle with Nona, but, because of Nona's age, had kept any sharp retorts to herself, Farran could not see how she could be missing any verbal combat. She hadn't thought she had enjoyed exchanging caustic comments with him all that much, anyhow.

Deciding that, in the main, she was a peace-loving person, Farran for no reason suddenly fell to thinking that she had been more placid than peaceful when it came to her relationship—or-non-relationship—with Russell Ottley. Then, suddenly, startlingly, it came to her out of the blue that although she had raced home from Hong Kong barely able to think of anything but Russell Ottley, for days now she had not given him one single solitary thought!

Hardly able to credit that, in under a month, she should go from feeling so unhappy to discovering that she was spending more time thinking about another man, Farran decided it was time to make Nona's porridge.

She went down the stairs still feeling slightly incredulous. Though when she pondered on how she had been thinking of Stallard before her thoughts had glided on to Russell, she was certain that meeting Stallard Beauchamp and his astringent tongue so soon after her return to England could have nothing to do with making Russell fade so swiftly from her mind.

'Shall we go to the library to change my books?' asked Nona Irvine at breakfast.

'Yes, of course,' Farran replied.

Later on, though, while at the library, she found Stallard Beauchamp an annoying source of anxiety. She had determined not to give him another thought, yet, as Nona took an age to select fresh library books, and the time neared when last week Stallard had arrived, Farran caught herself constantly looking at her watch.

'You're speeding!' Nona complained with one of her usual up-front back-seat-driving remarks on the return journey.

'I'm not, actually,' Farran replied evenly, but she could have saved her breath, because Nona had gone on to her next instruction.

'Watch that car!'

'I'm watching it.'

'You're much too close!'

There was no sign of Stallard's car when they returned to the smart well-to-do area where Nona had her home. Inside the house Farran made coffee and, realising that Stallard could not be intending to pay Low Monkton a visit that weekend, felt sure it made no dif-

ference to her personally. Nona would have enjoyed
seeing him, though.

Once coffee was out of the way, Farran left Nona with
her library books and went to make a start on the lunch.
She feared she was feeling out of sorts again as she
washed lettuce and prepared a salad.

Maybe she should have accepted Tad Richards' invitation out, she mused. Not that she had any particular
interest in Tad, but an outing with him occasionally
might help break up the tedium of her three months in
exile.

Nona for once insisted on giving her a hand with the
washing-up after lunch, and Farran was once more a
little ashamed that she had parcelled her in with her
thoughts of the tedium of her present existence.

'I can finish up in here now,' Farran smiled as Nona
dried the last plate.

'Then I'll get back to things dark and murky,' Nona
replied, and disappeared back to the detective fiction of
her library books.

Thinking it likely that Nona would be cat-napping
inside ten minutes, Farran stayed pottering in the kitchen
so as not to disturb her. Her thoughts were on how un-
harmoniously she and Stallard had washed up the lunch
things together last Saturday, when—drat the man! she
thought crossly, because it was quite beyond her why he
should keep popping in and out of her head that day.
As if she cared! She didn't! She didn't care if he never
took the time and trouble to come and visit a poor, sweet
elderly lady... Farran's thoughts came to an abrupt halt
at that point. Nona Irvine might be elderly, but she was
not poor, and was more inclined to be tart than sweet.
Which, Farran realised, made her wonder how much
truth there was in any of the rest of her cross thoughts.

She was just having one of 'those' days, she decided. Quite honestly, she did not give a button if she never saw Stallard Beauchamp again.

Which honest thought made it stranger than ever when, in the sitting-room an hour and a half later, she should glance through the windows and feel her heart suddenly begin to flutter wildly.

'Here's . . .' she broke off to clear her throat. 'Here's Stallard,' she told Nona as she recognised the long, sleek car she had once journeyed in as it purred silently up the drive, and then saw the tall, commanding figure of Stallard step from it.

'Oh, good!' Nona exclaimed, and struggled as quickly as she could out of her chair. 'You go and put the kettle on while I go and let him in,' she instructed.

In the kitchen, Farran heard the murmur of voices as she set the kettle to boil and began to lay a tea tray. Her heart by then had ceased behaving idiotically, and was beating normally, but as the kettle boiled and she made a pot of tea, she was visited by the oddest feeling of being shy to see him again.

Living alone with Miss Nona Irvine must be sending me potty, she mused as she checked that all they would need was on the large tray, for she could never remember being particularly shy of company before.

Having therefore just told herself to stop being ridiculous, Farran just could not account for the breathless sort of feeling that swamped her when, before she could carry the tray into the sitting-room, Stallard suddenly appeared in the kitchen.

'Hello,' she greeted him quietly, feeling shy again.

'How's your world?' he enquired, with a half-smile which she decided she liked very much.

She recalled how she had started off in complaining mood when he had telephoned last Tuesday. 'Can't complain,' she told him, with a half-smile of her own, and as her full smile made it, 'How's your world?' she asked him.

She saw his eyes go to her mouth, then, warmly, his eyes returned, to remain steady on hers. 'In no need of improvement,' he murmured, and her breath caught. Because, although she was not fully sure, it seemed to her that he had not been talking of 'his world' but of—her. To shatter that illusion, however, he moved his glance from her and, his voice level, queried, 'Is this tray ready?'

'I can take it,' she told him, knowing she was wasting her breath because he already had the tray in his hands, but needing to say something to cover the oddest sensation of—was it disappointment?—that he had not in any way meant his remark personally.

'Lead the way,' he instructed.

Farran led the way, and, as Nona graciously poured tea, and tea and dainty cakes were handed round, she sat back while Nona engaged Stallard in conversation. She was grateful that Nona seemed to have stored up a week of bits and pieces which she wanted to relay to the son of Murdoch Beauchamp, for it gave her time to take stock of herself.

What was wrong with her, that she should inwardly know such unrest the moment he appeared? She didn't fancy him, for goodness' sake, of that there was no doubt! Why, more often than not he was a swine to her. So, unless she was a devil for punishment, why should she remotely fancy him?

Farran went deep into Russell Ottley territory to remind herself of the fool she had made of herself over him. She was, most definitely, not going over that course again—especially with a man who had a reputation for playing the field. At least, according to Georgia—and popular rumour—Stallard Beauchamp was a man who, while dodging all efforts to tie him down, had an eye for a beautiful woman.

'I'm sorry?' she apologised, realising that Nona had just said her name. 'I'm afraid...'

'I wasn't talking to you, but of you.' Nona gave her one of her rare smiles. 'I've just asked Stallard to stay, and reminded him how you worked hard last Saturday while we were out in getting a room ready for him.'

It was news to Farran that Nona was so much as aware she had been upstairs with a duster, for she had not commented on it. Farran was determined, however, in her recently endorsed opinion that she did not fancy Stallard, that she did not care one way or the other whether he went back to his own home that night or not.

'The room won't hurt for always being kept up to the mark,' she offered non-committally, when it seemed that Nona expected her to make some reply.

'You'd prefer I didn't stay?' Stallard asked point blank, though not looking in the least likely to break out in spots—nor looking in the least likely, for that matter, to do anything he did not want to do—should she voice a preference for his room rather than his company.

'How could I not want you to stay?' Farran smiled, and left it to him to sort out whether she was being sarcastic, or whether she was telling him that since it wasn't her house, she had little say in the matter anyway.

'How indeed?' he replied, but as Farran glanced at him she saw from the faint narrowing of his eyes that he read her answer as more challenging than non-committal. 'Which room is mine, Nona?' he then ignored her to ask.

Delighted that he had accepted her invitation, Nona told him, and would have sent Farran to put fresh towels in the bathroom had not Stallard told her he could see no need for any fuss.

'If you point me in the general direction of the linen cupboard, I can help myself,' he told Nona firmly.

'You're bossy, just like your father,' Nona told him with a fond smile, but she gave in on that score. 'Now what would you like for dinner?' she asked him. 'Farran is a first-class cook.'

'I'm sure she is,' Stallard replied smoothly, though managing to sound as if he didn't believe it for a second, 'but I'm sure too that she must have earned a night off. We'll have a meal out,' he decided, making Farran— who had never forgotten his 'quite—unbelievable' comment about her scones—doubly certain he was being offensive about her expertise with a stove.

'Farran too?' questioned Nona, startling Farran a little that she apparently wanted to include her in the meal out.

'I . . .' she tried to get in to say that she would have a bite of something at home.

'Naturally, Farran too,' Stallard buried her voice beneath his own. 'It's inconceivable that we'd dine without her.' Sarcastic pig! Farran fumed, and might well have erupted to tell him what he could do with his 'Naturally, Farran too', only, to her chagrin, he gave her no chance, but went on pleasantly to Nona, 'Now, since I need a fresh shirt, are you coming into town with me to help me choose it?'

Farran had to hand it to him after he and Nona had gone, Stallard had tremendous charm when he cared to use it. Not that he had bothered to use it on her, but when it went without saying that he needed no one's help in the selection of a shirt, Nona had been highly delighted that it seemed he would value her opinion.

In a 'blow the lot of them' mood, Farran went upstairs and washed her hair, drying and brushing it until it shone a glorious dark brown, then went and surveyed her wardrobe. The cream two-piece with the red silk blouse was perhaps neither understated nor overstated, she thought.

She was still up in her bedroom when she heard Stallard and Nona return. But, in defiant humour, instead of going downstairs to see if she was needed, she went over to her bedroom chair and began leafing through a magazine.

When conscience prodded that Nona was sometimes more arthritic than others, though, her defiant state of mind began to weaken. And when she heard Nona come slowly up the stairs, and then heard sounds of her moving about in the next room, Farran could not hold out any longer, but went to see if she needed a hand with anything

'Why, how pretty you look!' Nona—able to manage all right on her own, so she said—exclaimed.

Farran returned to her room and went to take a look in her bedroom mirror. Her hair was newly washed, true, but she had not a scrap of make-up on, and the blouse she had slipped on after washing her hair had seen better days. She moved away from the mirror, trying to remember if Nona had been wearing her glasses, but, since Nona's compliments were few and far between, glasses off or on, she had to admit that she felt a little cheered from Nona's observation.

Dinner that night was not a huge success. At least, from Farran's point of view it wasn't. The meal in itself was faultless, as was the hotel restaurant which Stallard took them to. But the whole time Farran was conscious of a growing enmity between herself and him.

She had long since given up wondering how things had deteriorated since her shy 'Hello' of greeting, and told herself that she didn't give a damn anyway that every word Stallard had uttered since then seemed to be more loaded with sarcasm than pleasantness.

When she had meant to be early downstairs, she had somehow managed to be the last one down. So that both Stallard and Nona were waiting for her when she hurried from her room.

She saw his eyes do a quick appraisal of her shape and appearance in her cream suit, and felt a wild urge to hit him when, rocking back slightly on his heels, he remarked, 'Scarlet suits you.' He had turned to escort Nona through the door before Farran could find a sharp answer. But, having for a moment earlier in the day believed there was the innuendo of a compliment to be seen in his remark, 'In no need of improvement', she did not make the same mistake again. She was in no doubt whatsoever then that Stallard was not saying that the colour red became her, but, because of what she had told him of her love for a married man—regardless that she had also told him it had come to nothing—he was saying that the colour generally associated with immorality—scarlet—was the right colour for her to wear.

Swine! she fumed, but was grateful that the good manners instilled in her during her formative years stood up, and that when for courtesy's sake Stallard included her in the conversation from time to time, she was able to remain outwardly polite to him.

Given that she and Stallard had a mutual dislike of each other, though, they had partaken of a first course and then a second without one sharp word from either of them. But a minute later the strength of her good manners was to be stretched to extremes. The dessert course had been brought to their table and conversation had lapsed for a few seconds. Farran had opted for apple pie to finish with, while Stallard chose cheese and biscuits. Nona, having eaten well, but with ever-avid appetite, had chosen a particular favourite—lemon meringue pie.

'My, this is good!' she exclaimed with relish as she dipped her spoon into the lemon meringue for a second mouthful. Suddenly, though, she was showing a sensitivity which Farran had not suspected she possessed when, lest her previous remark offended, she halted mid-spoonful and added quickly, 'Of course, the one you made when your young man came to lunch was every bit as...'

'Which young man would this be?' Stallard broke in sharply.

'Andrew,' Nona replied. 'Quite a pleasant man, I thought.'

For once it appeared that Stallard was not a bit interested in what Nona thought. But turning from her, he looked with icy eyes at Farran and demanded harshly, 'Who invited him?'

'M...' Almost, Farran hurled, 'Moby Dick—who else!' back at him. Almost too late, however, she managed to get control of her overstretched good manners. 'You don't object, surely?' she asked in her sweetest, if slightly strained tone.

She was saved any stinging or sarcastic answer when, clearly missing the sparks that were flashing between two pairs of eyes, Nona came in to state blithely, 'I invited Andrew. I thought it would be nice for Farran.'

Smiling a 'pick the bones out of that!' smile, Farran looked at Stallard, expecting to hear something short and sharp from him to the effect that she was supposed to be spending three months in purgatory, not entertaining her men friends at cosy lunches.

To her surprise, though, for all his tone was as acerbic as she expected, he showed complete indifference to the matter under discussion, and changed the subject totally, by asking curtly, 'Have you found a new cleaner yet?'

As Farran remembered it, he had told Nona to advertise for a cleaner. 'I'm—working on it!' she told him, and cut into her apple pie.

She was glad to get back to the house, and when Nona gave a genteel little yawn and said she thought she would go straight to bed, Farran collected up anything Nona wanted from the sitting-room and went up the stairs with her.

When she had left Nona, Farran contemplated going to her own room. She had no idea how long Stallard intended to stay downstairs—not that it was important; he could rot down there for all she cared. But habit, no matter how recently acquired, died hard, and instead of going to her room she tripped lightly down the stairs and, making for the front door, was just about to slide the bolts home when the sound of Stallard's voice stopped her.

'I'll lock up!' he grunted from somewhere behind her.

Farran turned round and saw him standing, tall, and loose-limbed, eyeing her from the sitting-room doorway. 'So long as you don't think I'm falling down on my duties!' she told him sourly, and went briskly past him and up to bed.

The dislike they had of each other smouldered away the following morning. She asked him if he was staying to lunch, and he, at his sarcastic worst, told her she could uncross her fingers, for, although she might have got used to cooking lunch for three, she could count him out.

'I wish!' she muttered, with a beautiful picture in her mind of him flat on his back in some boxing ring, and was grateful when he took Nona out for a short drive.

They came back around midday, and having escorted her into the house Stallard went back to the car to collect a paperback book purchased on the trip, but which had fallen from Nona's lap on to the floor of the car. 'Stallard says he'll get on his way now,' Nona remarked as, having shed her hat and coat, Farran walked with her into the sitting-room. Before Nona could reach her usual chair, though, her right eye suddenly decided to water, and she discovered that she hadn't got a handkerchief.

'I'll get you one,' Farran volunteered, knowing exactly where to find them, since this was not the first time Nona had found herself handkerchiefless.

Hoping Nona could cope with her runny eye while she was gone, she went swiftly upstairs and speedily into Nona's room. With equal haste she went over the chest of drawers and extracted a handkerchief. Hurriedly she closed the drawer and, turning about, circumnavigated Nona's bed, and was swinging out through the bedroom door when she was sent reeling backwards as she crashed straight into Stallard striding along the landing towards his own room.

'Why the hell don't you look where you're going?' he blazed, by some good fortune grabbing hold of her as she very nearly fell.

'Why the hell don't you...?' she began to retaliate, when, suddenly, the feel of his hands on her arms caused her to start to tingle, and she forgot entirely what she had been about to say. 'Why—don't—you...' she tried again, but the heat of sudden anger had gone, and she was feeling breathless all at once—and it had nothing at all to do with her cannoning full tilt into the manly size of him.

Something seemed to be happening to him too, she thought hazily. At any rate, all harshness had gone from his expression and from his voice as he asked softly, 'Why don't I—what, Farran?' And then, as the hands on her arms began to draw her inexorably closer, there was no need for words. Suddenly they were in each other's arms, and as if in desperate need of each other they were locked in a hungry, passionate kiss.

Farran had never known such a sensation as the one that rocked her to feel Stallard's warm and searching mouth over hers. As the kiss broke apart, all she was capable of doing was looking at him, stunned.

She was not sure she did not gasp out loud, but whether her eyes that looked into warm grey eyes were showing how stunned she felt, or what they showed, she had no idea. All she knew for sure was that she was glad when Stallard seemed to need no encouragement, but lowered his head and kissed her again.

Farran knew more delight, for, not content with enthralling her with his kisses, Stallard began to caress her back and shoulders. She felt him press her close up against him, and she voluntarily, purely because she wanted to, moved closer to him.

His mouth was still over hers when she became partly conscious that they were both moving, but she was in a trance where nothing else mattered but the feel of his mouth over hers. She was nonetheless a little shaken when as his mouth left hers and he trailed kisses to her throat, she opened her eyes to find that they were in his bedroom!

'Stallard,' she murmured huskily as he pushed the neck of her sweater aside so his lips should gain access to the warm skin beneath.

'Farran,' he responded, and moved with her again, this time nearer to his bed. Warning bells were starting to go off in her head when his mouth returned to claim hers, and as one hand caressed to cup her right breast her right hand clenched in an anguish of wanting.

The backs of her legs were against his bed when a sudden lucid moment visited, and had to be grabbed at while she still had a vestige of control. For all at once she realised that there was material in her right hand, and the material which her fingers were clenched hard on was Nona's handkerchief.

At that moment, however, Stallard started to move with her down to the bed, but it was then that Farran took avoiding action. She owned that she felt too mixed up to know whether it was fear that Nona might have grown desperate for her handkerchief and might come upstairs and find them that was responsible for her action, or if it was from some last-moment strength of mind. But, whatever it was, she couldn't have said then whether she was glad or sorry that, when she pushed at Stallard in an attempt to get away from him, he should suddenly still, then look deep into her eyes and then— let his arms fall to his sides.

Whether the confusion she was feeling was visible to him she had no way of knowing. But he was still looking deep into her eyes when, taking a step back from her, he exclaimed, 'Good lord!' and, as if he just didn't be- lieve it, though at the same time somehow knew it for the truth, 'You—don't—*ever*?'

Farran swallowed hard, and, realising what he was asking, 'N-never,' she replied, and took a shaky breath, and found an even shakier smile, to try and quip, 'I'm— er—saving myself.'

There was no answering smile on Stallard's face, she observed, and he had moved a couple more paces away from her when, recovering from any incredulity he had suffered at his discovery of her virgin state, he replied suavely, 'I hope the lucky man you marry appreciates it.'

Swallowing again, Farran turned and fled.

CHAPTER SEVEN

FARRAN felt restless after Stallard had gone. She rather thought she had cause to feel restless too—because never had she known she was capable of feeling such emotional passion as had taken charge of her when he had taken her in his arms.

It was no wonder to her, therefore, that she could not get him out of her head for the remainder of the rest of that Sunday, and for all the following day.

She began to feel a little troubled, though, when the next day dawned and Stallard was still in her head. For by rights, the memory of him and his kisses should have begun to fade by now, surely?

'Whose turn is it this Tuesday?' Nona asked over breakfast, and Farran realised things were improving, for not only was Nona's question pleasantly asked, but she discovered that she was right on her wavelength in that she had no need to ask what she was talking about.

'Lydia Collier's, I think,' Farran replied, and went back to her thoughts of Stallard.

He was in her head again that afternoon when, having delivered Nona to play bridge at Lydia Collier's house, she made her way back to await Nona's phone call to come and collect her.

Reaching the home she shared with Nona, she was still wondering why on earth she couldn't get Stallard out of her head as she entered the sitting-room—when suddenly she stopped dead. Clutching desperately on to the back of a chair as if it was a lifeline, she was not sure she did not lose some of her colour. With stunned movements she made her way to collapse into the chair as she tried to take in what had happened. For all at once, in the quietness of the house, with no one there to interrupt her train of thought, a shattering truth had come to her.

Indeed, so shattering was it that she was unable to take it in at first. But, as she went over her thoughts again, and recalled how she had been thinking of his reference to 'the lucky man you marry', she suddenly knew, unquestionably, that she wanted *him* to be the man she married!

Thirty minutes later Farran was still trying to get to grips with this revelation that had come to her unbidden. She had tried telling herself that it could not be, and that she was in love with Russell Ottley, so how could it possibly be? But it had taken no thinking about for her to realise that, in comparison to what she felt for Stallard Beauchamp, she had most certainly never been in love with Russell.

Perhaps, she even tried to fool herself, having been infatuated with Russell, it was just infatuation that she felt for Stallard too. But she knew, with an inner conviction, that what she felt for Stallard was no mere infatuation. Nor was it just physical, nor something born out of the need she had felt for him when she had been in his arms. This love she felt for him, she acknowledged, had been coming on for some while.

Time ticked by as Farran, utterly stunned, acknowledged also that nothing could come of her love for Stallard. How could it? Apart from him being a man who rumour said 'never looked like settling down', he did not even like her, let alone love her! Oh, he might have kissed her, and might have desired her too, but basically he still thought of her as a money-motivated woman—and nothing she could say or do was going to alter that.

She was in the middle of realising that her pride was such that she would in no way beg him to change his opinion of her, when the phone rang.

'Can you come and pick me up, Farran?' asked Nona.

Glancing at her watch, Farran saw with astonishment that for hours she had been mindless to anything but the discovery of her love for Stallard. 'I'll come straight away,' she told Nona quickly.

Finding that she was in love with a man whom she had told herself she hated altered little, Farran found, as Tuesday gave way to Wednesday, and Wednesday gave way to Thursday. For life went on for her in the same routine.

True, Nona was less cantankerous than she had been initially. But she still had what Farran had grown to call her 'fetch me' days, when, instructed to go and fetch her cardigan, or her easier shoes, or her writing paper and envelopes, Farran would run up and down stairs on her errands.

'I need some more knitting wool. We'll go to the shops,' Nona announced on Friday, and Farran suddenly realised that the old lady, who had been a little achy this last two days, must be feeling better, for she had not been interested in her knitting while her arthritis was 'playing up'.

Farran too started to feel better that evening, though since she had been without a physical ache or pain, she knew exactly why she was starting to feel more alive inside. The week had dragged by on leaden feet, but at last tomorrow would be Saturday. Would Stallard come?

Stallard did not pay them a visit that Saturday, and by the time she went to bed that night Farran's nerves were in shreds from listening out for every car that came near the end of the drive, and from her heart beating erratically every time a car stopped—before moving on.

She determined on Sunday that she was not going to go through the same mental torment that day. 'Would you like to go for a drive?' she asked Nona at breakfast.

'Stallard might pay us a visit while we're out,' Nona declined, so Farran stayed at home, only to go to bed that night with her nerves again stretched—for they had seen no sight of Stallard.

There was some light relief from her constant thoughts of the man she was in love with when nearing lunchtime the next day Dr Richards came to call.

'I'd have thought, this being Monday, that you'd be up to your eyes in Monday-morning ailments,' Nona said in her forthright manner as soon as Farran showed him into the sitting-room.

'It was my weekend on call,' he answered her with a smile. 'As a concession they let me loose when the clock struck twelve today.'

'So this isn't a duty call?' Nona asked him, her brain as alert as ever.

'Calling to see you was never a duty, Miss Irvine,' he parried, and asked, 'How are you?'

'I'd feel better for a visit from the son of an old friend of mine,' she answered.

Farran went to the door with the doctor ten minutes later, having realised that she wasn't the only one who felt brighter for Stallard being there.

'I've got two tickets for an absolutely splendid play!' Tad Richards told her in the hall.

'Oh, that I could come with you,' she smiled, and felt no compunction in using the excuse which Nona had just dropped into her lap, when she added, 'but Miss Irvine is feeling a little down just at the moment and I don't feel like leaving her on her own at present.'

'I haven't told you which night the tickets are for yet!' he exclaimed ruefully.

Farran felt stumped for a moment. 'Some other time,' she said, and opened the front door, not giving him chance to invent a date a week hence when she might well find that she had committed herself.

'I won't give up,' he grinned, and threatened, 'Expect to see me next Monday—and the Monday after that!'

As things turned out, Farran saw him before the following Monday. Though to start with everything went on much as the previous week, with the bridge session being held that Tuesday at Celia Ellams' home.

By the time Friday came around, however, Farran was hard put to it to hide her growing inner ferment. Because, and it seemed logical to her, since Stallard had missed calling at the house in Low Monkton last weekend, then surely he must call this weekend.

She was doomed to disappointment on Saturday, for he did not appear. By Sunday morning she was heartsick of waiting for him, and had Nona this time suggested that they take a drive after breakfast Farran was sure she would have found an excuse for staying at home.

But Nona did not suggest a drive, and, as lunchtime came and went her face was showing a little of what Farran inwardly felt—that the weekend was almost over and that, since Stallard had not visited, they would have to wait and hope to see what *next* Saturday brought.

'I think I'll go and have a lie-down upstairs,' Nona suddenly broke into her thoughts.

'You're feeling all right?' Farran enquired, not really alarmed because occasionally Nona did opt to take her afternoon nap on top of her bed rather than in her chair.

'Quite all right,' Nona assured her.

'I'll come up and get my book,' Farran told her, and the two of them went upstairs together.

In her room Farran collected her book from her bedside, and wondered, since she had not absorbed a word of the printed matter in her recent insomniac hours, how she thought she was going to get Stallard out of her head during the hours of daylight. It wouldn't be for the want of trying, anyway, she determined, and went from her room to halt suddenly and abruptly at the top of the landing. Was that a cry?

Swiftly she went to investigate, and entered Nona's room to see her holding on to the chest of drawers. 'I—had a little dizzy turn,' she said as soon as she saw Farran.

'How do you feel now?' Farran asked, hiding her inner alarm.

'Perfectly well,' Nona declared, but allowed Farran to lead her to sit down on the bed.

'Do you hurt anywhere?' Farran asked quietly.

'No,' Nona smiled, but, unwittingly disturbing her companion, went on 'Though I think I'll get into bed, rather than lie on top.'

Fifteen minutes later, having helped Nona into bed and having been told that there was nothing that she wanted but half an hour's nap, Farran made her way downstairs. In the sitting-room she put the disquiet she felt against Nona's assurances that she now felt fine, and found that the two did not balance—disquiet proving greater than assurances. Seconds later, she was on the phone to Tad Richards.

'I'm sorry to ring you on a Sunday afternoon,' she began, and recounted Nona's dizzy turn and how, unusually, although she had said that she felt perfectly well, Nona was now voluntarily tucked up in bed.

'I'll come and take a look at her,' he said easily. 'I'll be there in five minutes.'

True to his word, five minutes was all that it took him. Farran was watching out for him and, not wanting him to ring the doorbell, when Nona might think it was Stallard, only to be disappointed, she had the door open as Tad Richards left his car.

'I haven't told Miss Irvine that I've asked you to call,' she warned him as he stepped over the threshold.

Nona was awake when they went into her room, and Farran discovered that Tad was more than able to cover that she had felt sufficiently alarmed to call him out on a Sunday afternoon.

'What are you doing to me?' he teased as he approached her bed. 'Here am I, come to ask the lovely Farran if she'll dine with me tonight, and what does she tell me but that my other favourite lady is feeling under the weather!'

'There's nothing wrong with me,' Nona protested, but all the same she did not demur when he said he might as well listen to her heart while he was there.

'As sound as a bell,' he pronounced when his examination was over. 'Though, since it isn't every day you have a dizzy spell, it could be that your body's requesting a little bed rest. Are you going to humour me and stay in bed for a few days?' he asked her.

'I—might,' she replied, and closed her eyes.

'Is she really as sound as you told her?' Farran asked him anxiously when she saw him out.

'She'll go on for years yet,' he promised, 'though, like the rest of us, she's bound to be unwell from time to time. And since it seems that she's a little overtired, bed's the best place for her. Now,' he said, taking off his professional hat, and donning his man-about-town image, 'are you going to make a liar of me, or are you coming out to dinner with me tonight?'

Farran smiled. 'How can I dine with you, Tad?' she asked. 'I couldn't possibly leave Miss Irvine while she's indisposed.'

'What have I *done*?' he asked, clutching his forehead.

Her smile had disappeared when she made her way back up the stairs. Tad had indicated that there was nothing wrong with Nona other than she was overtired, but Farran still felt uneasy.

'I'm not asleep,' Nona told her, opening one eye as Farran appeared in the doorway.

'How are you feeling?' Farran asked.

'If you're going to fuss, I shall get up,' Nona told her, though, worryingly for Farran, there was none of the waspishness in her tone which the elderly lady would once have used.

'So I'll stop fussing,' Farran smiled, and asked, 'Do you want to sleep, talk, or shall I get you a cup of tea and a biscuit?'

'Talking of eating,' Nona took up, 'are you going out to dinner with Dr Richards tonight?'

By that time Farran had realised that if she gave Nona the same excuse for not accepting his invitation as she had given Tad, Nona might well do as she had promised a minute earlier, and leave her bed.

'No,' she shook her head, and as Nona looked at her, clearly expecting more, Farran, since it no longer hurt any more, was able to tell her honestly, 'I recently came off second best over a man,' and, a little less honestly, 'I can't find any interest in the male sex at the moment.'

'Love can be a bind,' Nona observed, sounding as if she spoke from experience, then promptly closed her eyes and went to sleep.

Leaving her room, Farran returned downstairs and did her best not to worry over Nona. She'll be all right, she told herself, hadn't Tad Richards said so? Against that, though, Nona was being too—well, if not exactly meek and mild, not herself either.

Her worries over Nona niggled away when later Farran went upstairs, saw that she was awake, and decided to stay awhile for a chat. But Nona did not want to chat, and that was pretty near unheard-of!

Farran might well have been able to have contained her worries. But when in the early evening she took Nona up a meal only to later find—when Nona's appetite was always phenomenal—that she had barely touched it, Farran started to grow seriously worried.

For about half an hour she wondered what she should do. The obvious thing to do was to ring Stallard, she supposed, but she did not want to do that. Tad, then? But what for? He'd been once not so many hours ago—and Nona's condition hadn't changed greatly since then. Nona hadn't eaten her dinner, though—and that was unheard-of!

At the end of half an hour Farran knew it was not Tad Richards whom she should ring but, reluctant though she was to make the call, she ought, since it was Stallard who was employing her to be with Nona, to ring him.

Oh, grief! she thought, and felt cross with herself for her dithering and cross with Stallard that he should make her a ditherer. She dithered no more, however, but taking control of herself, went and found his number, then went over to the phone and dialled.

'Beauchamp,' a well-remembered voice answered.

'It's—Farran,' she managed, after a pause during which the whole of her felt like so much jelly, and she had to jerk yet more control into herself.

Another pause followed, then, as Farran drew a controlling breath to be ready to tell him what she had to, Stallard was questioning toughly, and sounding for all the world as though he had no recollection of once holding her passionately in his arms, 'What do you want?'

'For me—nothing!' she told him coldly, feeling hurt to the quick that, quite plainly, while she had ached for him the past two weeks, he did not give a hoot about her. 'I'm just ringing to tell you that Nona is unwell.'

'You'd be better ringing a doctor, I'd have thought!' Stallard whipped back sharply in her ear.

'The doctor's already been!' Farran hurled straight back, too hurt by his cold, impersonal manner after the warmth they had shared to be hesitant any longer.

'So what's wrong with her?'

'She's overtired, and in need of bed rest!' Farran thought that just about covered it and, the hurt in her peaking, she slammed down the receiver.

Swine! she fumed, not for the first time, then cooled down to wonder—what had she expected, for goodness' sake? He was a man of the world, for crying out loud, and as such he was probably so used to kissing and leaving that he never gave the women he left behind a second thought—much less paused to remember those warm intimate moments.

Farran went upstairs reminding herself how she had known Stallard would never love her. She went into Nona's room, aware of the sad fact that just because her day started and ended with him she could not hope that it was the same in reverse for Stallard.

'Now,' she smiled brightly at Nona, 'would you like me to sit with you for a while?'

When Farran went to bed that night, she was marginally less worried about Nona than she had been. For it seemed to her that the old lady had recovered some of her former spirit. At any rate, she had recovered sufficiently to have discovered a dozen and one things which were downstairs, and which she would prefer to have near at hand.

Feeling physically tired, Farran finally settled Nona for the night and went to her own room feeling mentally wide awake. Having retrieved her book from Nona's room, she then spent the next half-hour in a determined effort to get into the plot. It was not possible, though, because there was a part of her that seemed equally determined that she should think only of Stallard and how, after the way they had kissed and clung, *surely* he could have been a shade warmer to her on the phone.

Damn him! she fumed when he first refused to budge out of her head. Sighing, she put her book down. It was a certainty that she wasn't going to be able to read that night, so she might just as well lie down and try to get some sleep.

She had just stretched out a hand to put out the bedside lamp, though, when suddenly the sound of something hitting the windowpane caused her to halt. She was still staring blankly at the window when the sound came again.

Denying her foolish racing heart, Farran knew it just couldn't be Stallard throwing gravel up at the window to attract her attention. Although, as she got out of bed to investigate, it did not surprise her at all that he was the first person she thought of—since he was always in her head anyway.

Shrugging into a fluffy pink dressing-gown, she pattered to the window and looked out. Then her foolish racing heart had its head. For at the sight of the tall man standing there looking up, joy entered her heart.

Abruptly she came away from the window and, tiptoeing downstairs, fought to get herself under control.

Joy still filled her heart, even if her tone was shrewish, when, having unbolted and unlocked the front door, 'I suppose you've got good reason for rousing decent folk from their beds!' she greeted Stallard as he stepped through the open door.

'Quaint!' he murmured as he stood looking down at her in the light of the hall.

Farran turned quickly away from him and, not wanting their voices to float up the stairs and disturb the sleeping Nona, she instinctively ducked into the kitchen.

She was still trying to puzzle out whether Stallard had meant that her old-fashioned greeting was quaint, or if he thought the sight of her without a scrap of make-up on was quaint, when she observed that he had followed her into the kitchen.

'You're not expecting supper, I trust?' she maintained her shrewish attitude to question, but was taken aback when he replied mockingly, 'Would I dare?' She had set the kettle to boil to make him a cup of coffee before she knew it. 'It occurred to me,' Stallard went on, his voice even, suddenly, all mockery gone, 'that since you must have been nursing Nona all day, in fairness I should come and take over night duty. I'll get a nurse in tomorrow,' he was going on, when quickly Farran cut in.

'A nurse won't be necessary,' she told him hurriedly.

'It won't?' he queried.

She hurriedly relayed what had taken place when Dr Richards had called, and related Dr Richards' prognosis. 'I didn't mean to alarm you when I phoned,' she went on, as she realised that she must have done just that for Stallard to have left his home especially to make the journey to Low Monkton that night. The coffee made, she handed it to him, and then, as he started to drink it, she had a sudden lovely thought. 'You intended staying the night?' she queried, while trying to sound as if she didn't care one way or the other, though secretly hungry to savour as many moments with him as she could.

'I'm not sure how else I'd have taken over the role of night nurse,' he replied, but, to warm her heart, she could hear no hint of sarcasm in his voice.

'Do you still intend to stay, now that you know that—er—um—your night nursing skills are not required?' she asked, hoping and praying.

'Would you turn a man out on such a night?' he asked, amusement pulling at the corners of his mouth.

From what Farran could tell, there was nothing wrong with the night, and her lips twitched too. She saw Stallard's eyes go to her mouth, and suddenly she sensed danger. All he had to do was reach out for her, and she would be lost—she knew it.

'It's nothing to do with me whether you go or stay,' she told him primly, and, although she wanted to stay down talking with him, she turned about. 'I'll lock up and...'

'I think you can safely leave that to me,' Stallard murmured. 'I've got to get my bag from my car anyway.'

'Goodnight, then,' she bade him.

'Goodnight, Farran,' he replied quietly.

Her heart had still not settled down when, having gained the upstairs landing, she paused in her stride. It was then that she realised there was a third person awake in the household that night. For suddenly Nona's voice was floating out to her.

'Was that Stallard I heard arrive?' she questioned.

'Er—yes,' Farran replied, and, realising that Nona must have brilliant intuition, and then some, she said, 'He's just getting his overnight bag from his car, then he'll be up. I expect he'll pop in to have a word with you before he goes to bed,' she suggested, and asked, 'Do you need anything, Nona?'

'Not now,' Nona replied. 'Goodnight, dear.'

Farran slept better that night than she had for a couple of weeks. She was up early the next morning, however, and raced around getting bathed and dressed. Stallard had a long drive in front of him, and she wanted to see him before he left to go to his office in London.

As early as she had arisen, though, she discovered as she went lightly down the stairs and into the kitchen that Stallard had arisen earlier. Not only had he got up early, she observed, as she saw he was ensconced in the kitchen drinking coffee, but from the newspaper he was reading—not one they subscribed to—he had already been out and about.

'Good morning,' she bade him as evenly as she could, as he lowered his paper and looked at her.

'Good morning,' he responded, and as she went over in the direction of the kettle she glimpsed that he was again immersed in his reading.

Finding that he had thoughtfully refilled the kettle for her, Farran switched it on, started the porridge cooking and began to lay up the bed tray for Nona. She found an egg-cosy in one of the drawers, and in between giving the porridge a stir she set about boiling an egg, while at the same time she wandered about making Stallard's breakfast.

Flicking a glance at him, she saw with a start that he was no longer reading his paper but was watching, as if in some fascination, her every movement.

'Er—what time are you leaving?' she asked, to cover an absurd moment of shyness.

She loved him all the more when, idly, he drawled, 'Trying to get rid of me?'

That was the last thing she wanted. But, since he must never know how much he meant to her, how much it meant to her, to see him, she searched, and found just the right note when mockingly she asked, '*Would* I?' Having, she hoped, conveyed that it mattered not a scrap to her whether he was there or not, she felt able to lightly add, 'It's just that, with your having a business to run...'

'I should hope,' Stallard cut in to drawl, 'that the business could survive for a couple of days without me.'

Farran's heart leapt wildly about within her at the thought that, by the glorious, most beautiful sound of it Stallard might be hinting that he was going to stay at Low Monkton for a couple of days, and she had the hardest work in the world to keep her face impassive.

She thought, though, as she busied herself loading up the bed tray, that she had just about managed it.

She concentrated hard on the bed tray, and, deciding it just needed a finishing touch, she reached to take one of the 'oddment' flowers from a vase on the kitchen windowsill and, popping it into a much smaller vase, completed the tray setting.

Taking hold of the tray, she was about to go from the kitchen when, perhaps because Stallard had carried a tray from the kitchen for her before, she found that she was pushing it in his general direction and telling him, 'Here, make yourself useful—take this up to Nona.'

She knew the moment she had said it that he was going to tell her to go to blazes, or something similar. For as clear as day, Stallard was a man who took orders from no one.

Then suddenly he was moving his long length from off his chair, and was all at once standing, all commanding, over her. She saw his eyes go to the tray, his glance taking in the flower she had just placed on it. Then, as her heartbeats thundered and she waited to hear something sharp and cutting, he flicked his eyes away from the tray and looked straight into her brown eyes.

Quietly then he commented, 'Pretty,' and her heartbeats thundered more loudly, so that in the emotion of the moment she could do nothing to stem the warm colour that flushed into her face. She saw that his all-encompassing gaze had missed nothing of her blush, as he drawled lightly, 'I meant the breakfast arrangement.'

In next to no time Farran was looking elsewhere. 'What else?' she snapped, and would have turned away had he not placed a finger under her chin and forced her to look at him.

'Were I talking of you, however, my dear Farran,' he commented as with wary brown eyes she looked into the grey of his, 'then I'd have used the word "beautiful".'

Her heart gave another tremendous leap at what he had just said, and she felt her heart would never beat normally again. Though how, with so much going on inside her, she managed to sound cool, she did not know. But, as she turned her head and the contact with his finger under her chin was broken, it was she this time who drawled, coolly, 'You're still making your own breakfast!'

Her heart was still on a merry-go-round when to her utter enchantment she heard him laugh. The sound of his amusement was still in her head minutes after he had picked up Nona's tray and taken it up to her. Naturally Farran cooked him breakfast!

She was happily alive to his being under the same roof in all she did in the following few hours. She was aware of him downstairs making a few business phone calls when, upstairs, she went into Nona's room and asked how she was.

'As fit as a flea,' Nona declared, and threatened, 'I think I'll get up.'

By dint of much persuasion and a promise of her favourite lemon chicken for lunch, Farran, having made Nona comfortable and got her to agree to stay in bed, went back downstairs.

She was in a sunny mood as she tidied and dusted the sitting-room, and had not one cloud on her horizon when later, in the kitchen, she sat writing a shopping list. She was still deep in lemon chicken ingredients when Stallard came and joined her in the kitchen and, to set her heart racing, came and stood looking over her shoulder at what she was doing.

'Is all that for today?' he enquired.

'Just a few supplies,' Farran told him, instantly realising that he would have no idea that having a man in the house unexpectedly—but more than welcome for all that—required extra shopping.

'I'll do the shopping for you if you like,' he volunteered, and even as Farran guessed—since he had probably seldom, if ever, visited a supermarket—that any shopping he did might be a disaster, she smiled.

'I'm sure Nona would prefer that you went and kept her company,' she replied tactfully, and saw from his grin, his wonderful, superb grin, that he wasn't fooled for a minute.

Because her shopping that day was a little more special on account of their special guest, Farran was out longer than she had intended. But once her shopping was done she drove home with an anxiety to return which had never been there before. It was not, she was honest enough to admit, on account of Nona.

As was usual after shopping trips, she unloaded the car at the front door. This time, though, in her eagerness to be inside the house again, instead of then driving the car into the garage she parked it alongside Stallard's car, intending to garage it later.

She forgot about the car once she had entered the house, however, for the sound of voices coming from the sitting-room told her that Nona had tired of her bed and that, even at the risk of having to forfeit a lemon chicken lunch, she had got up.

Dumping her shopping in the kitchen, Farran went on to the sitting-room and, while as aware as ever of Stallard sitting opposite Nona, she questioned with mock severity, 'Is it any good telling you that you'll rest better in bed than you will down here?'

'I've had all that from Stallard,' Nona smiled, and was totally unrepentant as she asked, 'Am I on bread and water for lunch?'

At which Farran had to laugh, and as she headed back to the kitchen she heard Nona starting to explain how she had tried to use bribery and corruption to get her to stay in bed that day.

Lunch was one of the happiest meals Farran could ever remember. Nona ate heartily and the conversational ball was passed freely. Occasionally, and probably because she was aware of every movement Stallard made, Farran would catch his eyes on her as she listened while Nona addressed some remark to her. Fear of him guessing how things were with her, though, caused her to limit the times she glanced at him.

Her cup of happiness was full to overflowing, however, when, as Nona went off to her favourite chair in the sitting-room when the meal was over, Stallard began to help clear the table.

'I can do it,' she thought it polite to protest, and discovered he could be as tactful as she when he retorted,

'Where would I go, if I'm not to disturb Nona's forty winks?'

Farran was in seventh heaven when Stallard stayed with her in the kitchen; so in love with him was she by then that she felt too choked up inside to find a topic of conversation. But she had no need to worry that there might be any long, painful silence, for, in the nicest possible way, Stallard was telling her that since neither she nor Nona had apparently done anything about getting some domestic help, he had that morning phoned in an advert to the local paper.

'There's no need!' she protested.

'There's every need,' he replied, and Farran, who knew that the house was as clean as a new pin, realised that he was not complaining that the house was dirty, but that house cleaning was not the job he was paying her to do.

Remembering the cheque he had given her, though, set her wondering if he would likewise pay the wages of the cleaning woman. Did he, in fact, pay all the household bills? It was a question she could not ask him.

Then he was sending all thoughts out of her head on the subject of Nona and her apparent need for nothing that money could buy, by asking levelly, 'Would it be impertinent to ask if your friend Watson has been to lunch recently?'

Feeling slightly startled, for she could not remember that it had ever bothered Stallard before whether he was being impertinent, Farran swallowed any sharp word which might break the beautiful harmony she was experiencing with him.

'It was only a one-off—that time he came to lunch,' she replied. 'I probably won't see Andrew again for another year or so.'

'Does that bother you?' asked Stallard.

It was on the tip of Farran's tongue to ask him if he did not have female friends on whom he looked more as sisters than woman friends, but she realised that would be a naïve question—of course he didn't. But she still wanted that harmony with Stallard, so she simply told him, 'I regard Andrew in the same light as I'd regard a brother—if I had one.'

There was a short pause as he dissected that, then, 'You're an only child?' he enquired, and the rest of the washing-up and the clearing up of the kitchen was completed with Stallard asking questions about her and her family, and with Farran asking questions too.

When the kitchen was put to rights and they went to join Nona in the sitting-room, however, she had learned little more than she knew already. From what she had been able to work out, though, Stallard, if her sums were right, was thirty-six years old. His father, he had revealed, had married late in life, and had been fifty when Stallard had come on the scene. He had died six years ago, and had been eighty when he had died.

'I must have nodded off,' Nona smiled as she heard them come back into the sitting-room. 'Now where did

I . . .? Be a dear, Farran,' she broke off to request, 'and run upstairs for my knitting bag. I . . .' she broke off as just then the front door bell sounded. Farran was on her way to answer it before anyone could stop her.

'Tad!' she exclaimed, opening the door to find the doctor standing there. 'How kind of you to call to see Miss Irvine!'

'Kind nothing,' he grinned. 'I've a couple of theatre tickets burning to be used. Don't you think . . .?'

'This way,' Farran broke in before he could finish, and led the way to the sitting-room.

She had the sitting-room door open when he tried to halt her. 'Farran,' he pleaded, 'give in—we could have a late dinner after the play,' he was saying as she went in.

Looking across at Nona, Farran smiled as she told her cheerfully, 'Dr Richards has come to see you!'

She stepped to one side and, as Tad put on his professional hat and went into the room, Farran thought that since all eyes would be on the doctor she could safely glance at Stallard. Immediately she did so, however, she froze. For Stallard was not looking at Tad Richards, but, his expression arctic, was looking nowhere but at her. Feeling stunned by the murderous glint she saw in his ice-cold eyes, Farran realised that, quite clearly, any feeling of harmony she had imagined to be between them was over.

Totally bewildered as she was by this sudden change from harmony to hating, she looked away. What, she wondered, had she done now?

CHAPTER EIGHT

FARRAN was still bewildered to know what she had done to cause Stallard to give her such a killing look, when she heard Nona introduce the doctor to him. She was still trying to get over the change in Stallard when, introductions over, apparently, she became vaguely aware that Tad was putting a few questions to Nona. But so shaken was Farran that she had not the strength to be more than just a mere bystander.

So much for her foolish belief that the enmity between her and Stallard was at an end! How crass she had been to think, for a moment, that just because she had seen none of his brutish side that day, she might never again see that side of him.

Farran had to push her hurt and mystification behind her, though, when it penetrated that Tad was on the point of leaving. 'I wish, Miss Irvine, that some of my fifty-year-olds were in such good physical condition,' he told his patient when, without need of a stethoscope, his eyes and the answers she gave him were all he required to know that she had no lingering effects from her dizzy turn of the previous day. 'I'll look in again,' he told her as he went towards the sitting-room door.

Farran moved in that direction too, obeying a natural courtesy to see him out. She could not resist casting another glance in Stallard's direction on her way, however, but at the look of icy arrogance he bestowed on her she quickly looked away.

Her heart was in her boots as she went out into the hall. She hadn't imagined it then, Stallard did hate her! 'About these theatre tickets——' Tad turned to mention as Farran opened the front door.

'Ring me,' she told him, giving him more encouragement than she had intended, but Tad Richards and his theatre tickets the last thing on her mind just then.

'You're on!' he exclaimed, and went off looking as happy as Larry.

Farran wished she felt the same as she closed the door after him and took a couple of steps towards the sitting-room. Suddenly, though, she halted. Something, she knew not what, was stewing up inside Stallard, that was for sure. But although she knew he had more class than to attack her verbally in front of Nona, she did not think she could return to the sitting-room and just sit there as if entirely unaware of the hate vibes he was aiming in her direction.

More by luck than judgement, she remembered that prior to Tad Richards' call, she had been on her way upstairs to collect Nona's knitting bag. Not that to collect a bag of knitting was going to take more than a few minutes, she mused as she started up the stairs, but at least it would afford her a few minutes in which to get herself under some control. She owned that she still felt extremely shaky.

It took no time at all to run the knitting to earth, but just as she had left Nona's room Farran heard the sound of the sitting-room door closing. Abruptly she stopped, then, certain that she heard Stallard's tread, but with no wish to meet him, she quickly dived inside her own room.

She was about to close her bedroom door when she heard his purposeful tread coming up the stairs, and hurriedly, not wanting him to hear the sound of her door closing—and thereby know where she was—she came away from the door.

She was the other side of her room when she heard his footsteps cease. Her breathing ceased too. Even as part of her demanded to know what she was afraid of, for goodness' sake, Farran held her breath as she waited for his footsteps to resume and for him to go past her room and on to his own.

But he did not go past her room, and her eyes were glued to the half-open door when suddenly it was aggressively pushed inwards. Then, while she was gaping in astonishment, Stallard, his look one of fury, was not waiting for an invitation but with a couple of long strides was in her room. A moment later he was standing no more than about five feet from her.

Nor was he waiting for her to speak first, but, his words as icy as his look, he demanded, 'So this is where you're skulking!'

Farran took a gulp of breath, but, having been figuratively knocked sideways in the last ten minutes, she was glad to feel the adrenalin of her own aggression start to pump. 'Skulking?' she challenged, and finding sarcasm too, 'At a guess—though I'm sure you'll correct me if I'm wrong—I'd have said that I've more right to be in my room than you—uninvited,' she tacked on.

'You're more free with your invitation to Richards, I assume!' Stallard rapped back, making her catch her breath. How did Tad Richards get into this?

'Some men are more pleasing than others!' she snapped, her adrenalin in full flow. By no chance was she going to back down—not now!

'I've noticed,' bit Stallard, the narrowing of his eyes showing Farran that he wasn't liking her answers. Nor, however, was she liking what he said when in the next breath he accused, 'It may have escaped your avaricious attention, but you're here to be a companion and a help to Miss Irvine, not to call her physician in at any time of the night or day to relieve your boredom!'

'Relieve my...' For a second Farran was totally bereft
of speech at what he had just said. Nor could she quite
believe her hearing. Then, 'How dare you?' she raged
when she had her breath back. 'You know full well that
I only phoned Tad because...' She broke off when
Stallard took a violent kind of angry step nearer.

'Tad, is it?' he snarled.

'Yes, it is!'

'Now isn't that terrific?' he gritted before she could
add more. 'While anything could be happening to Nona,
you and *Tad* play lovey-dovey in the hall!'

'That's untrue!' yelled Farran, but she discovered, as
Stallard's hands snaked out and he caught her upper
arms in a fierce hold, that she was wasting her breath.

'How many times have you been out with him?' he
demanded, and, while Farran was realising that the
reason Stallard was so furious was that he thought she
left Nona on her own night after night, 'Have you forgotten why you're here?' he barked toughly.

In actual fact, since Farran had grown to like Nona,
the reason why she was there acting as her companion
had started to become dimmer and dimmer in her mind.
But she suddenly saw no reason why he should know
how she had almost hung out of the window looking for
him this last two weekends. 'Fat chance of that,' she
retorted angrily, 'with you always on the doorstep!'

He didn't like that, she could tell from the way his
jaw jutted and the fierce grip he had on her arms
tightened. 'You'd rather I stayed away, of course,' he
gritted. 'By being here, it's clear I see too much of what's
going on,' he snarled, and while she was chewing on
that, 'If I hadn't been here today,' he went on grimly,
'I should never have known that—to the detriment of
an old lady—you're doing a nice little line with her
doctor.'

'That's unfair!' Farran erupted.

'Is it?' Stallard challenged, and, looking at him, Farran saw that his jutting chin, his grim, steely-eyed look, told her plainly that she could argue until she was blue in the face, but he would still believe what he wanted to believe.

But she was still angry enough not to ever want to back down, and since she saw it as a waste of breath to try and convince him that he was wrong, all she could do was to let out a frustrated, 'Oh—go to hell!'

She saw at once, however, that she'd have been better not to have said anything at all. For plainly, as Stallard's brow shot back, he had not liked her remark. Plainly too, as she witnessed the way his face became a mask of aggression, no one told men like Stallard to go to hell and got off lightly. She had evidence of that the instant he started to draw her closer.

'No!' she cried in panic, but she knew her protest was useless. Any minute now she was going to be made to pay for her remark.

It happened sooner than that. One moment she was struggling to get out of his grip, and the next she was pulled hard up against him, and his mouth was over hers.

There was no gentleness in his kiss, only fury. In silent combat Farran fought to be free. 'No!' she managed to cry again when his mouth came away from hers for a moment. But her release from his mouth was only momentary, and then his mouth was over hers again, his lips seeking as, with a strength that far outmatched hers, he moved her where he wanted her to be.

That that place just happened to be her bed caused her yet more panic. 'Stop!' she demanded as he pressed her down to the mattress, but she was such a mass of contradictions inside by then that her voice was barely audible.

Stallard did not seem to have heard her protest, at any rate. Or if he did, he chose to ignore it, for, as his mouth claimed hers in angry capture, he effectively prevented her from wriggling her body away from him by half lying on top of her.

All the same, Farran tried to wriggle away from him, but only to hear, as her body moved hard against his, that all she was doing was to fan the flames of desire in him. 'Keep that up, sweetheart,' he gritted, 'and I might yet rape you!'

'Huh!' she scorned, but it was sheer bravado, and she was aware that he would know it when, immediately, her body stilled beneath his.

Suddenly, though, some of his aggression seemed to go out of him, and yet strangely, as his harsh kisses gentled—almost in apology—Farran discovered that she had ceased fighting; that the will to fight had gone out of her.

She wanted to tell him 'No' again, she knew that she did, but when gently he kissed her again, she just seemed to lose all idea of what it was she wanted to say.

'Stallard!' she breathed softly instead when he broke that gentle kiss, and then, as suddenly warm grey eyes searched melting brown ones, his hold on her became tender.

'Farran,' he spoke her name hoarsely, and then his mouth was over her mouth, his lips parting her lips. Then he was transferring his kisses to the side of her face and placing a gentle warm hand on her throat.

Wanting his mouth on hers again, Farran, without conscious thought, wrapped her arms around him. She felt the hand at her throat caress slowly down to her breast, and she clutched at him in an uncontrolled movement.

Then his mouth was over hers again, and as she freely gave him her lips and arched to get closer to him, she heard him groan. She was lost to everything save him, and gave him kiss for kiss, exhilarating in the feel of him as his lips sought her throat and he traced tender kisses behind her ears.

The next time his hand caressed her breast, Farran gave a small cry of shock. For, without her being aware of it, so busy had she been in returning his kisses, Stallard's fingers had unbuttoned her shirt and his fingers were inside her bra.

Desperately, as passion soared in her, she gripped hard on to him. She had no demur to make though when, finding her bra an encumbrance, he undid it. A sigh of pleasure escaped her as his right hand fitted, as though made for that purpose, over her left breast. 'Stallard!' she cried huskily, wanting him with all her being when his mouth left hers and he bent his head, his lips capturing the hardened pink tip of her breast.

Farran was in a mindless ferment of wanting when, while his hand and mouth caressed over both her breasts, his other hand went to the waistband of her trousers. Then, however, when there had been no thought in her head to deny him anything, she was suddenly caught out by shyness when she felt his hand warm on the flat of her belly.

She had no need to worry. For whether she made a small instinctive movement which Stallard read as rejection, or whether it was his intention all along to reject *her*, she was too confused to know. What she did know was that in the next second after she had felt Stallard's hand on her silky flatness—it was all over.

For a moment, as he abruptly took his hands away from her and rapidly jerked off the bed, she could not take in what was happening.

Stallard, however, did not leave her in doubt for long. 'Cover yourself up, Farran,' he instructed her lazily from his stance over by her dressing-table. 'We don't want to risk you getting pneumonia, do we!'

His tone as much as anything, like a jet of cold water, was enough to bring Farran quickly to awareness. She glanced down to where her swollen breasts were exposed to his full view and, desperately, with no real clue to what was happening, she drew the folds of her shirt together and got up off the bed. She was buttoning her shirt when his tone, along with his sarcastic comment, started to register, and an ice-cold chill struck at her heart.

Even so, 'What...?' she had to question.

'My oath, Farran,' he drawled, as she stared at him blankly, 'did I make a mistake?'

Staring at him, hearing the mockery in his voice, Farran returned swiftly to reality. It was painful but true, she began to realise, that while she had been lost to everything but his kisses and caresses, Stallard had been lost to nothing but his decision to take her up to the heights, so that he could drop her flat.

'M-mistake?' she queried, as anger started to spark into life inside her.

'There was I assuming you were after getting your money-grasping talons into the good doctor,' he taunted. 'How wrong I was, dear Farran!' he jibed. But his tone was changing, and she heard aggression in his voice when, 'You're after fatter pickings than he can provide, aren't you!' he stated sharply.

Farran took a shaky breath, and could barely believe that after the tenderness they had just shared—as brief as that time had been—he could taunt her so. But the anger that had begun in her had started to spiral out of control, and suddenly she was stamping down her hurt, to erupt furiously, 'My stars! I wouldn't marry you, Stallard Beauchamp, if...'

'*Marry!*' he broke in, thunderstruck. 'Who the hell was talking about marriage?' he demanded, and while Farran could not help realising that marriage in his book was more alarming than exciting, he had recovered from looking as thunderstruck as he sounded, and was at his most ridiculing yet when he derided, 'Don't save yourself for me, sweetheart. I ain't the marrying kind.'

'You'd be...' Farran began hotly, but broke off when the sound of Nona's clear voice came floating up the stairs.

'Don't forget my knitting when you come down, Farran,' she called.

Looking about her, Farran saw the knitting bag which, although she had no memory of dropping it, now lay on the floor. Swiftly she went to retrieve it. Then she turned angrily to Stallard.

'Here,' she spat, 'you take it! I need to bathe your touch from me before I go down those stairs again!' With that, her actions accompanied by a seething look of hate, she pushed the knitting bag at him.

Momentarily, as she saw his jaw tighten, she thought her last remark had caught Stallard on the raw. But she knew she was mistaken when, taking the bag from her, he sent her a fairly murderous glance, then turned and left her.

Farran did not go and run a bath once he had gone, but stood there remembering how thunderstruck he had been at the horrifying thought of marriage. Why, oh, why had she brought marriage into it!

Awash with embarrassment, racked with pain, Farran felt stifled by her emotions. With her heart breaking, her pride took a hiding that Stallard must have known from her response that, given a natural shyness, she had been ready to give him her all. Worse, did he know from that, had he guessed, that she was in love with him? Oh, how could she ever look him in the face again?

Suddenly, at that moment, what pride Farran had left came to give her the answer. That answer—that she didn't have to look him in the face again.

In the next second she was getting out her suitcases. A minute after that she was throwing her belongings into them. Her thinking thereafter seemed to be in limbo when, by sheer physical effort, she saw to it that her cases did not hit against anything to make a sound as she carried them down the stairs.

She went silently past the sitting-room door, heard that the television was on, and hoped the sound would cover her exit. She thanked heaven that she had forgotten to put the car away, but she was many miles away from Low Monkton before the awful thought struck her—it wasn't her car. She had as good as stolen it!

A mile further on, and the fact that she had stolen the car—which, if memory served, Nona had told her Stallard had paid for—seemed the least of her troubles. A couple of miles even further on, and Farran started to surface from the pain and the heartbreak that was going on inside her.

By the time she reached Banford, though she knew she was still heart and soul in love with Stallard, she had found a stray wisp of anger, and was desperately calling him names. Swine! she thought, on a dry sob. It was his fault! He shouldn't have kissed her! He shouldn't have... Oh, damn him, damn him to hell.

Farran was opening the front door of her old home when, with a groan, she belatedly remembered that her head had been so full of Stallard that she had forgotten entirely about Nona.

A moment later, however, she was dredging up some hate against Stallard and was telling herself firmly that, since he had intimated that he could take some time off work when he wanted it, then he could jolly well take some time off work and keep Nona company himself.

'Farran!' her stepfather beamed the moment he saw her. 'How lovely to have you home. You are—er— staying this time, aren't you?' he queried.

'Yes, Uncle Henry, I'm staying this time,' she told him, as she gave him a hug.

She took her cases up to her room and tried to keep thoughts of Stallard out of her head by firstly cogitating if she should or should not write a note to Nona, and then secondly in guessing that Georgia was likely to kick up a fuss when she discovered what she had done.

To her surprise, however, when Georgia did arrive home from her beauty salon, Farran was to find pleasantly that some of the hard edges seemed to have gone from her stepsister.

'What are you doing back?' was Georgia's first questioned exclamation to her.

'I...' she began, and was suddenly so emotionally choked that, unable to go on, she just looked away from her.

'Oh, love!' cried Georgia; this was the nearest she had seen Farran to tears in years. 'This is much worse than that fella in Hong Kong, isn't it?' she questioned intuitively.

'You could say I've learned the difference between l-love and infatuation,' Farran replied a shade shakily.

'Who?' Georgia enquired.

Farran took a deep breath. 'Stallard Beauchamp,' she said his name, and knew that Georgia too saw the hopelessness of her loving a man like him, when,

'Oh, love,' she said again. Then, gently, she asked, 'What happened?'

'Not much,' Farran told her. 'We fought, we laughed, I fell in love with him—and I'm hoping with all I've got that he hasn't guessed how I feel, because, as you once said, he's not the settling-down type.' She paused to take a strengthening breath, then, loving her stepsister too, she told her honestly, 'I can't go back, Georgia.'

'I know,' Georgia replied, and looked thoughtful.

'You don't seem to mind too much,' Farran interrupted her stepsister's train of thought. 'I mean, this is bound to end any chance of getting Stallard to tear up Aunt Hetty's last will.'

'Mind!' Georgia answered, and with a glimpse of her former harder shell showing she said frankly, 'I mind like hell!' Then suddenly she softened, and, staring into space, quietly confessed, 'But between you, me, and—to quote Mrs Fenner—the gasworks, I'm rather gone on a certain fella myself, and where he's concerned I'm not acting very rationally either.'

Farran accepted that maybe Georgia was right in her opinion that she was not acting very rationally over Stallard. But, by the sound of it, Georgia was suffering some of the same trauma which she had been through.

'Idris Vaughan?' she questioned.

'He's the one,' Georgia confirmed.

'Doesn't he love you?'

'If he does, he isn't saying, and I'm sure as hell not asking,' Georgia replied, and, making a big effort, 'But to get back to our problem. There must be a way,' she opined.

'I'm not going to get in touch with Stallard again!' Farran told her quickly.

'I can see that,' Georgia replied with a smile. 'But, to get down to practicalities, do you really think he'd be so mean as to exact his full pound of flesh?'

'I'm not with you?'

'Well, you did stick it out with the old dear for a month,' Georgia pointed out, adding, 'Even a third of the inheritance would give me the purchasing power I need.'

As Tuesday and Wednesday came and went, Georgia was still racking her brains to think of some way they could claim what she declared was rightfully theirs. Farran owned that she was not much help to her stepsister. She had more pressing worries of her own, not least the car that had been standing on their drive ever since late on Monday afternoon.

Thursday came and went and she still had done nothing about returning it. Neither had she done anything about writing a note to Nona. She started to feel bad about that, but owned that she felt too defeated just then to want to do anything.

With black humour, it crossed her mind to wonder if anyone back at the house at Low Monkton had paused to consider that she was taking rather a long time in her bath. Glumly she realised that she wouldn't be missed all that much anyway. Nona thought the world of Stallard, and while he was there she probably wouldn't give anyone else another thought.

Proof, though, that someone knew she had vacated the bathroom at Low Monkton came the very next afternoon. Farran had been arranging some flowers in the kitchen, and had just reached the sitting-room and was putting a display down on a window table, when suddenly the phone rang.

'Hello?' she said, on going to answer it, and suddenly the deadness in her heart suddenly sprang to life.

For, 'You have something of mine!' hit her ears sharply.

Oh, dear heaven, Farran thought as she recognised Stallard's voice, and had to swallow hard before she could make any sort of reply. Her heart was racing like a wild thing when, gripping hard on to the phone, she answered stiffly, 'Tell me where you want it delivered, and I'll arrange it.'

'Are you being funny?' he demanded toughly, his tough tone firing more life into her.

'Do I sound as though I'm joking?' she retorted spiritedly.

'Oh, confound it!' roared Stallard, and the next Farran knew, he had slammed the phone down in her ear.

Confound you too! she fumed as she replaced her receiver, and was unsettled for the rest of the day. What the heck did he mean—Are you being funny?

She got up on Saturday morning and determined that she was definitely going to do something about that car outside today. Though, since she could not face returning the car in person, the next best thing seemed to be to employ someone else to do it. The only problem with that, however, proved to be the fact that, on a weekend, nobody wanted to know.

With her determination somewhat dented, it was nearing midday when Farran put the phone down after her last call. She was just resolving that she would most definitely set the ball in motion on Monday when the phone near her hand chirruped for attention.

'Hello,' she answered it, a trifle warily, she had to admit. Although she didn't really think Stallard would ring again.

Her relief was tinged with quite a bit of regret, though, when a female voice queried, 'Hello—Farran?'

'Nona?'

'How are you?' Nona queried, with not so much as an atom of censure in her voice for the way in which Farran had so abruptly walked out on her.

'Oh, very well, thank you,' Farran replied, and, because she had grown to like Nona, a warmth crept into her tones. 'Is everything all right with you?' she asked and quickly, 'You haven't had another dizzy turn or...'

'I'm as fit as a fiddle,' Nona declared, as Farran had learned, still holding the view that it was bad manners to be ill, and even worse manners to admit to it. 'I'm missing you, though, dear,' Nona, to Farran's surprise, went on, 'and I was wondering if perhaps you could come and have a cup of tea with me this afternoon?'

'Oh, I don't think...' Farran began to hedge, as she sought for tact.

'I know it's a long way to come for a cup of tea,' Nona broke in, and, alarmed, Farran was not sure that the old lady had not choked on a sob, before she gained control to tell her, 'I'm so lonely now that I'm on my own.'

'You're on your own?' Farran questioned swiftly.

'Stallard's found me a new companion, but she won't be here until Monday. And what with him going overseas, I shan't see anything of him for a month, and...'

'Stallard's—gone abroad?' Farran cut in to question, despite being determined not to.

'He went last night,' Nona confirmed, and suddenly, to Farran's ears, Nona was sounding not only lonely but for once, every one of her years, as she added, 'It would so cheer me if I could see you today.'

Farran weakened rapidly. So much so that, even as it came to her that if she went it would be one way of returning the car, she was saying, with a smile in her voice, 'Put the kettle on, dear, I'm on my way.'

She was too, Farran mused only a short while later. All she had stayed to do was to change into a dress rather than trousers, and trip along to the workshop to tell her stepfather where she was going, and to stop by the kitchen to have a few words with Mrs Fenner, then it was out to the car.

She tried not to think of Stallard as she drove along—it was certain that, in whatever foreign clime he was, he would not be thinking of her. In a moment when she did get him out of her head, however, Farran stopped to purchase a few flowers to take to Nona, and on her way again wondered with what frequency—since she would be returning by train—the trains departed from Nona's part of the world to her own.

Farran was nearing the end of her journey when it suddenly occurred to her to wonder how Nona had found her telephone number. Not long after that, she hit on the only solution that would fit. Stallard must have given it to her.

She pondered for a moment on why he would do that. But it did not take her long to work out that, since he clearly cared a great deal about the elderly lady, he had given her her phone number in order to make her feel a bit more secure while he was abroad.

Which, Farran realised as she drove into the village of Low Monkton, must mean that he had some idea that she too might have some feeling for Nona, and could therefore be relied on to find time to chat reassuringly to Nona for a little while, should she be called upon to do so.

A glow of warmth for Stallard washed over Farran as she drove up the drive to Nona's house. For a second or two she debated on whether she should park the car in the garage now, or later. Remembering Nona's tone, and how lonely she had said she was feeling, though, Farran decided that later would do. Nona might well have heard her pull up and be on her way to the front door anyway, she thought as, remembering the flowers, she took hold of them and left the car, and went to ring the front door bell.

She was still feeling a glow of warmth that came from thinking pleasant thoughts of Stallard when, with no sound of footsteps to be heard but as if Nona had seen her from the sitting-room and had gone to the door and was waiting only for her to ring the bell, the front door opened. And Farran almost fainted dead away. For the tall, upright person who opened the door was nothing like the person she had expected to see. For it was not

Nona but a man who, according to her information, had left England's shores last night!

'You!' gasped Farran, any warmth of feeling for him quickly disappearing.

'None other,' Stallard drawled coolly. 'Come in.'

CHAPTER NINE

GRIPPING the flowers she held tightly, Farran fought to get herself together. But she was so utterly flabbergasted to see Stallard that she was still all over the place. 'Wh-where's—Nona?' she asked on a gulp of breath.

Fear for the elderly lady entered her heart, though, when for a reply Stallard stretched out a hand and, since she had not yet accepted his invitation to come in, assisted her over the threshold. Farran supposed she must have been numbed to some degree that she allowed him to do so. He still had his hand on her arm, though, when, as she began to grow even more afraid that he must be there because Nona was ill, he led her into the sitting-room.

'Where is she?' she questioned, pulling out of his hold, her voice taking on an urgency when it was evident that Nona was not in the sitting-room.

'At this precise moment,' Stallard replied, his eyes steady on hers, 'I'd say she's happily engaged in a game of bridge.' And while Farran's eyes shot wide, 'She'll ring in about three hours when she wants a lift home,' he added evenly.

'But—but...' Farran shook her head as if hoping that would clear her confusion. 'But Nona's expecting me!' she exclaimed, and felt more confused than ever when:

'Correction,' he told her. 'I was expecting you.'

'You...?' she broke off as some part of her brain started to get clear of the fog that clouded it. If Stallard had been abroad—as he should have been—then if Nona had been ill, there was just not time for him to have been recalled and to get back in between now and Nona's phone call to her of a few hours ago! 'You're supposed to be overseas!' Farran recovered a little from her shock to accuse him coldly.

'As you can see, I'm not,' he replied, then, fixing her with a level look, 'Might I ask, Farran, why you refused to come to see Nona until she told you that I'd gone abroad?'

Swiftly she looked away, trying desperately hard to remember how her conversation with Nona had gone. 'I...' she began. 'You,' she amended, and by good grace found some stiffening to tell him hostilely, 'have nothing to do with it!' She saw a muscle move in his temple, but she sensed he was waiting, waiting for more, and found that his very silence was forcing her on. 'You may not believe it,' she added coolly, while trying to convey that she did not give a button if he believed her anyway, 'but I do have some regard for Nona, and...'

'Why, then,' Stallard interrupted her sharply, 'since you have some regard for her, did you run out on her the way you did?'

'I should stay around after the way you insulted me?' Farran erupted, and instantly regretted it.

But it was too late to blame his sharp tone for drawing her heat, or to blame her inner turmoil for her speaking without first thinking, because an alert look had come into his eyes, and he was looking at her very thoughtfully indeed.

'Then I do figure in this somewhere, you'll agree?' he questioned slowly.

'I'll agree that from where I'm standing, it looks to me as if you and Nona have set me up!' Farran snapped edgily. 'Though why you should go to the bother of that is beyond me. Not,' she said quickly, coldly, when it looked as though Stallard now wanted to interrupt, 'that I'm remotely interested in your reasons.' She was heading for the door when she remembered the flowers she still held. 'Here,' she pushed them at him, 'give them to Nona with my compliments.'

'Give them to her yourself!' barked Stallard, not ready to take this sort of treatment from anybody, she saw as, with chips of ice suddenly in his eyes, he was all at once there between her and the door—effectively preventing her escape.

'If you think I'm hanging around here for another three hours, you've got another think coming!' Farran refused to be browbeaten by his look of hostile aggression. 'If you'll get out of my way,' she charged on, her words tumbling out one after the other, 'I've got a train to catch!' That thought triggered off another, and as nerves started to get to her, she just couldn't stop. 'You can have your car keys too!' she told him for heated, speedy good measure as she dipped into her bag to find them. 'I never did intend to keep the car, so you could have saved yourself a phone call yesterday...'

'I didn't ring you yesterday about the bloody car!' Stallard sliced in thunderously—about the only way he could get in to break her flow. 'Ye gods, what the...'

'You could have fooled me!' Farran flared, wishing he would move away from the door, yet feeling too nervous suddenly to try and force the issue by going any closer to it.

Strangely then, though, when it was she who was the one feeling nervous, she saw Stallard take what seemed a deep and steadying breath. His voice was much more even, and much more quiet, when after a moment or two he said, somewhat mysteriously, she thought, 'I've fooled myself for too long—the fact I've fooled you too hardly surprises me.'

Farran was unsure what to make of what he had just said, though since her head, her emotions, seemed to be all over the place, all she could do was to stand and stare at him, and hope he might clarify his statement.

She was not quite sure, though, that she really wanted his clarification when, as he stared into her eyes, he suddenly suggested, 'Shall we sit down? I'm sure you'll be far more comfortable...'

Before she could agree or otherwise, he had taken the car keys from her and put them and the flowers on a table. Then, as if intent that she should be seated, he touched a hand to her elbow. Instantly Farran moved away from him and went over to one of the easy chairs in the room.

She thought she saw what might have been a hint of a smile cross his features when, glad to feel the chair beneath her, she decided she might as well sit for a minute or two. Any sign of a smile had left him, though, when he took the easy chair opposite.

When he began to speak, however, he did not, to her surprise, explain or refer in any way to what he had meant when he had said he had fooled himself, but instead began pleasantly, 'It was something of a shock to me on Monday, when I returned from a walk in which I'd endeavoured to get certain matters into perspective, to discover that the car had gone from the drive and that...'

'I've brought the car back,' Farran reminded him stiffly, while at the same time she noted that he had not, as she had thought, been watching TV with Nona when she had gone past the sitting-room with her cases, but had taken himself off for a walk.

'Would you please shut up about the damned car,' Stallard requested, which, since he had this time mentioned it first, Farran thought was most unfair. 'As I was saying,' he went on, ignoring the cold look she tossed him, 'or was about to say, before you interrupted,' he amended, 'it was a shock to me that you'd gone. A shock to me that you'd walked out heedless of the risk that the inheritance you were working for...'

'I don't care about the inheritance,' Farran interrupted yet again.

Stallard did not this time tell her to please shut up, but instead fairly bowled her over when quite categorically he stated, 'For yourself, you never did.'

'How...' she began abruptly, as she looked across at him. Then, more slowly, 'How do you know that?' she questioned.

'Do you think I go around with my eyes closed?' he counter-questioned, and when Farran was not in to answering that 'There's been nothing mercenary or premeditated in the way you pitched in here from the start,' he told her. 'You didn't have to clean the place up—it wasn't what you were engaged to do, and yet...'

'Good grief!' Farran cut him off, starting to grow annoyed that on top of everything else he thought of her, he seemed to think she would happily live in a pigsty. 'Even women after "fatter pickings" have some degree of fastidiousness about the condition of their living accommodation, you know!'

Immediately she had said it, Farran wished she had not reminded him how, the last time she had seen him, he had accused her of being after 'fatter pickings' than Tad Richards could provide.

But, when she was determined to stay angry with Stallard, he was suddenly cutting the ground from right under her feet by saying—and there was no mistaking his sincerity, 'If you'll allow me to, I'll apologise, not only for that vile remark, but for every other remark I've made that's hurt you.'

It was on the tip of her tongue to retort that in that case it looked as though they would be there for an age. But, in time, she realised that to say anything of the sort would surely give him some indication that he did indeed have the power to hurt her.

'So,' she said after a few moments' thought, 'am I to take it that you no longer think I raced back to England with all speed from Hong Kong to claim my third of what Aunt Hetty left?'

'You don't have an avaricious bone in your body,' Stallard again shook her by making another categorical statement. Though his expression darkened as he asked harshly, 'Do you still think you're in love with him?'

'Who?' she questioned warily.

'The man you ran from in Hong Kong. Ottley, the man you were so down about at Miss Newbold's funeral that I, in my superior wisdom,' he inserted with a self-derisory shrug, 'mistook it for an insincere display of grieving for a woman you'd never bothered to visit in the time I'd known her.'

'I...' Farran began, and felt weak inside. Hurriedly, though, she found some backbone, and coldly told him, 'It's none of your business whether I'm still in love with Russell Ottley or not. For that matter,' she added decisively, 'I can't see any reason why I should hang about now that Nona's not here!'

With that, she got smartly to her feet. She had only made it as far as the settee, though, when Stallard, moving faster, caught her by the arm. She was taken off balance, and all he needed to do was to give her arm a small tug—and Farran found she was sitting on the settee next to him. More, when he saw she had no intention of staying put, he gave her a no-nonsense sort of a look and held her there.

Sparks were flashing from Farran's eyes as she opened her mouth to give forth. But Stallard again proved the quicker. 'Hell's teeth!' he ground out, 'I haven't gone to the lengths I've gone to to get you here purely so that you can walk out! I want to talk to you,' he gritted. 'I need to talk to you. I . . .'

'So ring me!' Farran blazed.

'I tried that!' he roared, but suddenly his voice had gone very quiet, but she clearly heard him just the same, when he added, 'It came out—all wrong.'

It was his quieter tone, his quieter look, that look which something in her crazy head read as his again being unsure of his ground, that caused the aggression and anger in her to die. While he was harsh, angry or sharp with her, she could match him. But she was in love with him—loved him so very much that, even if it would be to her own detriment, her soft heart would not allow her to say, 'Tough!'—which was what she knew full well she should say.

'What,' she asked firmly, while without undue haste taking her hands out of his grip, 'exactly went wrong?'

'What,' he replied, 'went right? From the very first, I got you all wrong.'

'I knew that,' Farran murmured, and was glad suddenly that she was sitting down, because the chances were that she might otherwise have fallen down from the shock of hearing Stallard admit what he just had. 'But—but when did you—er—realise—that . . .'

'It was obvious almost from the beginning,' Stallard told her. 'The trouble was, though, that time and again, just when we seemed to be getting on well, you had to go and make me angry.'

'*Me* make *you* angry!' Farran flared, having soon lost any softness over his sensitivity. 'I'm supposed to sit meek and mild while you . . .'

'There was never anything meek and mild about you, Farran Henderson,' Stallard cut in. 'Those beautiful brown eyes of yours were emitting angry sparks on the first occasion I spoke to you. I well remember your haughty look, your . . .'

'*My* haughty look!' Farran exclaimed. 'My god-fathers,' she charged on, having never forgotten that occasion up in Aunt Hetty's bedroom when he had come in and found her looking for Aunt Hetty's will, 'you could give lessons in arrogance!'

'Arrogant? Me?' queried Stallard, and she could have thumped him. She refrained, however, and softly he murmured, 'It must be the effect we have on each other.'

But Farran wasn't sure she liked that any better. For certain she didn't want him getting the idea that he had any effect on her whatsoever. Yet to say so, she feared, would be giving the matter too much importance. She thought she had better get him off the subject.

'You were saying—about...'

'I was trying to apologise,' Stallard corrected her. 'I was trying to explain,' he went on, but suddenly he halted, then seemed to be choosing his words most carefully, when he continued, 'why through circumstances that were—new—so new—to me, I've been so brutish to you.'

Never ever having expected to hear him admit such a thing, Farran shot a glance at his face. Suddenly her eyes went wide. For in the grey eyes that steadily stared back, there was the warmest look. 'Oh,' she said, and had her life depended on it she did not think she could have added another word.

But she did not have to add anything. For, with his eyes still warm on hers, and almost as if nothing would do but that he made a full apology, Stallard took her back to before they met, when he revealed, 'Matters were in some degree of confusion when Miss Newbold died. No one seemed to know where any of her family lived, and with Nona becoming stressed that her bridge partner might not have all due respects paid to her, I came down to see what was to be done. I subsequently learned that a Mrs Allsopp cleaned for Miss Newbold, and arranged for her to do anything that needed doing in the domestic line prior to the funeral. It was Mrs Allsopp who gave me the tin containing Miss Newbold's personal papers, and it was then that I saw not only the names and address of her family, but discovered from her latest will that I was her sole beneficiary.'

'You—didn't know until then?' Farran found her voice to enquire.

'It came as a complete surprise,' Stallard told her. 'I realised at once, of course, that Miss Newbold had changed her will in my favour on some whim, but before I took steps to have that will quashed, I . . .'

'You intended to have that will quashed!' Farran exclaimed. 'Even before I rang you and . . .'

'I'm afraid I did,' he confessed openly.

'Then—then,' Farran spluttered, 'Georgia needn't have checked you out or worried. And I—I had dinner w-with you for nothing. I came down here and w-worked for . . .'

'It wasn't quite so simple as that,' Stallard told her quickly, seeing she had gone from being an attentive listener to starting to look angry. 'I thought, at first, since Miss Newbold had gone to the trouble to get that will legally documented, that I'd a duty to her to first make some enquiries to see if there was some good reason why she should disinherit her kin.'

'You made enquiries about us!'

'I didn't have to,' he replied, and added, 'Forgive me, Farran, but I thought I could safely bet that I wouldn't have to do much other than wait. I was convinced that either directly, or through solicitors, I'd soon be hearing from one of the three parties named in her previous will.'

'So you weren't surprised when I rang and left a message with your secretary that I'd like you to ring me back?'

Stallard shook his head, but then, to astound Farran, he told her, 'You and I had already met at Miss Newbold's funeral, and I confess I was not too displeased at the thought that I might see you again.' Farran's heart leapt at that, and her eyes were glued to his as he went on, 'Yet when I returned your call and knew you were lying about having not seen the date on the will, I discovered to my great surprise that instead of being annoyed by such deceit, I was actually enjoying myself.'

'You—were?' she asked, still feeling shaky inside and striving hard to get herself together.

'To start with, I was,' he confirmed, and further confessed, though more slowly this time, 'In actual fact, I'd had you on and off in my head since the funeral.' Farran swallowed, hoped he had not witnessed her emotional moment, and waited for him to go on. 'You'll have to forgive me again, my dear,' he said quietly, the soothing look in his eyes, not to mention that quiet 'my dear', causing her such havoc that it was only by the strictest control that she saved herself from swallowing again.

'Oh?' she questioned as evenly as she could. 'Why?'

'Because as I thought of you, it was my feeling that it wouldn't be a bad idea to make you jump through a few hoops for your neglect, and your family's neglect, of Miss Newbold.'

'I see,' Farran said slowly, as her heart resumed a dull beat that Stallard had not after all been thinking of her as her, but of her in relation to making her pay for the fact that none of her family had visited Aunt Hetty in her last year of life. 'Well, you came close, didn't you?' she added stiffly. 'As I remember it, you found a way to make me "jump through a few hoops" when I told you that not only was I jobless, but I got on with elderly people.'

'Be fair to me, Farran,' Stallard asked her quietly. 'My reasons for what I did seemed sound at the time. I did, in actual fact, need a companion for Nona. Maybe I was in error, but it seemed to me that since you wanted your inheritance, there was no good reason why you shouldn't knuckle down and work for it.'

'Thanks!' Farran snapped coldly, and in the tense pause that followed she was minded to get up from the settee and to make a more determined effort this time to leave.

Before she could take any such action, however, Stallard, his tone deliberate, was telling her, 'If it's any consolation, you soon had me not knowing if I was on my head or my heels,' and as her eyes rocketed to his and she forgot all about leaving, he gently took hold of her hands in his, and added, 'So many things about you began to warm my heart.'

'Don't!' Farran cried in sudden alarm, and while her heart raced in panic she tried to snatch her hands out of his hold.

'Why not?' he asked quietly when, looking intently into her afraid brown eyes, he refused to let go the hold he had on her hands.

'Because... Because... Damn you!' she flared, but she could see she was getting nowhere. Then she became aware that the look Stallard had in his eyes was gentle for her, was quiet for her, and seemed to her to be saying 'trust me, I won't hurt you', and suddenly she found she was overcoming her fears. 'Wh-what sort of things— began to warm your heart?' she asked breathlessly.

She thought he gave a relieved sort of smile. Though whether that was because he was relieved that she was not afraid of him, or—not that she could believe it— that he had gained encouragement from her inviting him to go on, she could not tell.

'Things such as the time when I called at your home prior to bringing you down here,' Stallard began. 'How could I not admire you when, even though I knew you were hating me like the very devil, your good manners held up in front of your housekeeper, as you asked if I'd like coffee?'

Farran's heart did a dizzy flip to hear him say he had admired her. 'It—er—seemed the natural thing to do,' she managed to murmur chokily.

'For you, and the lovely person you are, yes, it would be natural,' Stallard smiled, and while Farran started to lose track of what day, week or year it was, he was going on, 'We laughed on that journey, and I discovered I liked your laugh.'

'We weren't laughing at the end of the journey,' Farran said without thinking as she remembered—and wished she hadn't, because she had liked Stallard the way he was, and she was sure her remark would have changed all that.

'You'd caught me on the raw,' he said, but as he remembered too, to her delight he stayed warm and friendly as he explained, 'In my business a handshake's all that's needed for my word to be trusted over vast sums of finance. Yet here are you daring to question my word, not once but twice, over something which by comparison was only twopenny-ha'penny coinage.'

'Oh, dear,' murmured Farran as, with Stallard putting the fortune Aunt Hetty had left into the 'twopenny-ha'penny' bracket, she gained an idea of how she must have offended him. 'Are *you* going to forgive *me*?' she asked.

'I'll forgive you anything,' he replied warmly, but added shrewdly, 'Though I've since realised that pushing for something in writing wasn't all your doing.'

'It was the first time,' she owned. 'But Georgia...'

'No matter,' Stallard broke in with gentle charm, and there was a trace of a smile at the corners of his mouth when he added, 'Though I was annoyed enough with you to cut short my time here that Saturday.'

'You left earlier than you intended—because of me?' Farran asked wide-eyed.

Stallard nodded, and told her, 'I didn't like at all the fact that this female whom I barely knew should have the power to upset my equilibrium so.'

'Oh,' Farran murmured shakily.

'But,' he went on, 'I'd forgotten my annoyance with you when the following Saturday came round. There was no thought in my head of not visiting Low Monkton that day,' he told her, then added shatteringly, 'Without my knowing it, Farran, I wanted to see you.'

'You—d-did?' she stammered.

'I did,' he said. 'Although at that time I neither accepted that, nor the fact that, because of you, I started out for Low Monkton far earlier than I would normally have done.'

Farran coughed to clear a sudden constriction in her throat. She swallowed as she fought hard to keep her two feet firmly on the ground. 'I don't think you could have wanted to see me all that much,' she tried to deny what he was saying as she remembered that particular Saturday in question, and when he frowned, as if not sure what she was getting at, she reminded him, 'You were going to stay overnight, but didn't.'

'If you remember that, my dear,' Stallard answered, his frown fading, 'you'll remember also that the day degenerated from bad to worse.'

'Nona was a bit—demanding that day,' she murmured, as she tried to instil sense into her heart that insisted on frolicking happily just because Stallard had again called her 'my dear'.

'I don't know what got into her that day, but "demanding" is understating it,' he murmured. 'But I wasn't talking about Nona, but about how things between you and me went rapidly downhill that day. We'd started out with you spiritedly telling me to "get lost" when I'd as good as accused you of being idle all that week.'

'I remember.'

'I later apologised for that,' Stallard went on, 'and I quite enjoyed myself—until, as we tackled the lunchtime washing-up, I started to ask you about your time in Hong Kong—only to feel suddenly furious when you dared to tell me that you're not heartwhole.'

Farran blinked rapidly. 'You objected to my telling you I was in love with Russell Ottley?'

'Most definitely I did—strongly,' Stallard answered. 'Even if I didn't know why I should feel I'd just been served a body blow, I didn't like that piece of information one little bit.'

'Oh,' she said, as she tried desperately to cope with the cluster of emotions that were rioting around inside her.

'I tried, as I took Nona on a drive afterwards, to get things into proportion,' he continued. 'But she was being pretty hellish with her prattle about Mabel Armstrong having garden gnomes where garden gnomes should never be, and what with her opening the car door as we drove along when she wanted the window open, I was more than a little frayed around the edges when, not done with her demands yet, she gave me some idea of the basinful you must have had all week. I was just thinking of that, and admiring you and your patience with her,' he continued, 'when some man I took to be your married lover from Hong Kong phoned.'

'It was Andrew, my...'

'I know now—brother-type friend. But I didn't know then, and even while I was able to scoff that, dammit, I wasn't jealous who r...'

'Jealous?' she choked.

'That's the word I used, sweet Farran,' Stallard confirmed quietly, letting go one of her hands and stroking a forefinger down one side of her face. 'Even if at the time I was scorning the idea that any such word could be applied to me. Though, having come after you to question you about your male visitors here, I realised that I needed to get away and try and get my head back together.'

'I thought you left—that day—because you disliked me so much that a few hours under the same roof as me were all that you could take.'

'If that was the case, why then do you suppose I should wake on Sunday morning and wish I was back at Low Monkton?' Staring at him with saucer-wide eyes, Farran instantly recalled how that self-same Sunday morning she had scorned the notion that she was wishing he had not left. 'If that was the case, why do you suppose that the following Tuesday—when I'm fairly certain you'll answer the phone and not Nona—I should obey an instinctive need to hear your voice and ring this number?'

'You didn't—er—sound as though you wanted to hear my voice when you started.'

'I was feeling awkward,' Stallard confessed at once. 'For the first time in my life I was experiencing new sensations. Can you wonder that I didn't know where the hell I was?'

'I—um—suppose not,' she replied, not knowing where all this was going to end but, if her life depended upon it, having no intention now of stopping him—whatever the outcome might be. 'Did you—er—know where the hell you were when you came down the next Saturday?' she asked huskily.

'The devil I did!' he smiled. 'You and I were soon striking sparks off each other, and I was having to cope with the news that you'd entertained Watson to lunch, and having to pretend that, in answer to your question "You don't object, surely", you could entertain another dozen like him to lunch for all I cared.'

Quite desperately Farran wanted to ask, 'But did you care in any way?' but, with her heart racing like an express, she just didn't think she could take it if he had been leading her on and told her bluntly that care, even in the smallest degree, he did not.

So instead of asking what she wanted so urgently to ask, and drawing a veil over the fact that the next day they had passionately embraced each other, she murmured, 'You didn't—er—come down the next weekend.'

'You noticed?' Stallard asked gently.

'I—m-missed you,' Farran heard her own voice confess, and was enraptured when a look of loving tenderness came over Stallard's features.

'I missed you, my very dear Farran,' he told her, and his voice sounded throaty, as if he was under some very great emotion. Then slowly he drew her closer to him, and there was no thought in Farran's head of not meeting him half-way when gently, almost reverently, he placed a loving kiss on her mouth.

'Wh-what—are you saying?' she could no longer hold back from asking when, just as gently, Stallard broke his gentle kiss and pulled back to look into her melting brown eyes.

'Don't you know?' he asked, and went on to say the words that caused uproar in her heart region. 'I love you,' he confessed, and, as she gripped convulsively on to the hands that again held hers, 'I love you with all my being, my dearest love,' he told her. Then, while Farran was swallowing rapidly in the utter joy of the moment, 'You can't still be in love with Ottley?' he questioned, his tone growing strained. 'Am I totally wrong,' he went on urgently, 'to believe that you can't have been as responsive with me as you've been, and still love him?'

Staring at him, seeing and hearing the urgency in his tone, there was no way that Farran wanted to hold back, or could have held back. That Stallard had realised it just was not in her make-up to be warm and responsive with one man while still in love with another made her feel even warmer to him, as she replied shyly, 'Whatever else you got wrong about me, you got that bit right.'

'You don't love him?' he pressed.

'It wasn't until I knew what being in love truly felt like that I realised that what I felt for him was nothing but mere infatuation.'

By that time Stallard's hands had left her hands and were on her upper arms, and he was gripping her upper arms tensely when he demanded, 'So who is it that you're truly in love with?'

Farran stared lovingly into his face. 'I'm looking at him,' she whispered.

A moment later, as the anxiety cleared from Stallard's expression, the tense grip on her upper arms disappeared. A moment after that, and his arms were about her and he was holding her close against his heart, murmuring her name over and over again.

How long they stayed like that she had no idea. All she was aware of was the joy in her heart where there had been pain. Then gently Stallard was pulling back from her and looking deeply into her eyes, and for long, long moments they just sat and looked at each other.

'It's true?' he just seemed to have to question.

'That I love you?' Farran asked, and added when he nodded, 'Yes, it's true.'

That was when Stallard kissed her. It was a magical kiss, a wonderful kiss, and as her arms went up and around him they kissed and clung, and clung and kissed, both having known the pain of loving, but finding the salve they needed in each other's arms.

Some while later Stallard pulled back and, running a finger down her nose, murmured ruefully, 'In the interests of my sanity, I think perhaps we ought to talk.'

'Anything you say,' Farran sighed softly. She was aware that her colour was high, but since the cause of that was sitting not a yard away grinning unrepentantly, she didn't feel too embarrassed. 'We might start,' she said with an attempt at primness, 'with you telling me why, if you were missing me so much, you managed to keep away that weekend.'

'Did I tell you that you're the most delightful, adorable creature of my acquaintance?' Stallard threw in, and knocked her primness for six when he kissed her soundly and received a response that was far from prim. 'But to return to your question,' he muttered, putting a few inches of daylight between them, 'I didn't know at that time that I was in love with you. At that time, all I knew was that you were causing me some considerable irritation...'

'Irritation?'

'Who's telling this?' he growled, and seemed to adore her even more when she laughed. 'To resume,' he said, mock sternly, 'I was finding it most irritating that thoughts of you should persist in popping into my head unwanted. But, because I was determined to get you *out* of my head, I decided I'd leave it some while before I returned to Low Monkton.'

'Ah,' Farran chipped in. 'But on the Sunday of the following weekend I phoned you and told you Nona was unwell, and because of Nona you felt you had to come...'

'Nona,' Stallard interrupted, 'had nothing to do with it.'

'But... She didn't?'

He shook his head, and smiling warmly, he revealed, 'I came down here that Sunday evening purely and simply because hearing your voice on the phone had so unsettled me, I didn't know where the hell I was.'

'Really?' she asked, wide-eyed and loving him with every breath in her body.

'Oh, yes, my dear,' he told her tenderly, and added, a smile coming to his face, 'You, woman, have made a liar of me.'

'How?' she wanted to know.

'Quite simply, I covered my eagerness to see you by pretending I'd come down to relieve some of your nursing duties through the night, until I could arrange to get in a professional the next day. But,' he went on, 'I already knew that there was very little wrong with Nona, and that she certainly was not in need of night nursing, or the help of a professional nurse.'

'How?' Farran asked again.

'Because,' Stallard owned, 'I rang her doctor after your call, and heard from him that there was nothing to worry about in her condition.'

'Well, I...' Farran broke off, and then as it hit her that Stallard had truly arrived that Sunday because of her, and not Nona, 'I think that's the loveliest lie I've ever heard,' she told him dreamily, and, as he gently kissed her, she floated on cloud nine for a little while, then asked, 'Er—did I have anything to do with your decision to—um—have a few days off work?'

'Minx!' he said cheerfully, and told her, 'I could hardly believe my ears when I—who, I might tell you, barring flood, famine or earthquake, never miss some part of the day at my desk—heard myself intimating that I was going to take a few days off work. All, of course, as you've so rightly guessed, on account of you.'

'Ah!' Farran sighed, if she was dreaming, never wanting to wake up. 'I wish I'd known!'

'I wish I'd known myself what forces were driving me to act so entirely outside the person I thought I was,' Stallard murmured.

'You didn't know then that you—loved me?'

He shook his head. 'There's none so blind as those who are determined not to see,' he smiled. 'What I did see that Monday, although I'd witnessed it before, was the gentle, natural way you had when you were in conversation with Nona or doing anything for her. Then, as we all sat down to lunch, I became aware of an inner happiness that hadn't been there when you'd been out shopping. Only later, my love,' he told her softly, 'did I come to realise that I only felt that happiness when you were in the same room. Only later did I realise that my only happiness lay in being in the same room as you—for the rest of my life.'

'Oh, Stallard!' Farran cried, and, thinking that the most beautiful statement she had ever heard, she leaned forward and kissed him.

All was silent for some minutes after that. Then Stallard was putting her away from him and, to her delight, was saying in a strained kind of voice, 'Ye gods, my darling, have you no idea what you do to me?' and when she grinned impishly, he added, 'I shall be deaf to the phone when Nona rings if we carry on like this.'

'You were saying...' Farran strove hard to come down from the dizzy heights he had taken her to, to remember exactly what it was he had been saying.

'I was saying,' Stallard took up after a moment or two, 'that I'd felt inner happiness when we sat at lunch on Monday.'

'But—it didn't last, did it?' she questioned, as she recalled that shortly afterwards she had packed her cases, and had left, Stallard's changed attitude, not to mention his words and actions, being the cause.

'How could it?' he asked simply. 'I, who've no memory of ever being jealous in my life before, had just been served with more than enough to make up for lost time. If it wasn't Ottley, it was Watson; then, right under my nose, Nona's physician is trying to date you. I knew damn well from my conversation with him on the phone that there was no need for him to call at the house again unless requested—yet, not twenty-four hours after his last call, there he is calling again.'

'I saw you were looking fairly murderous,' Farran murmured. 'I wondered what I'd done wrong now.'

'Poor love!' groaned Stallard. 'Have I been such a fiend? Don't answer that,' he said quickly, then told her, 'I was in such a jealous rage about Richards daring to call you Farran—and that was before it registered that he'd come to see you, not Nona—that I just wasn't thinking straight. I most certainly wasn't thinking straight when I followed you upstairs and accused you of neglecting her.'

'You knew I hadn't?'

'Lord, yes,' he said emphatically. 'But at the time I was ready to accuse you of anything, I was so crazed. Though my decidedly unclear thinking wasn't helped when you intimated that it wouldn't bother you if you never saw me again—and on top of that had the unmitigated nerve to tell me to go to hell. Only later,' he ended, 'did I wonder what in creation had been in possession of me.'

'You—finally realised that—you care for me?'

'Care for, love, and adore you,' Stallard said tenderly. 'But I had to go through another four days of being furious with you and furious with myself, and spend the same number of nights for the most part sleepless and just thinking of you, before, yesterday afternoon, lightning struck.'

'Lightning?'

'A bolt of lightning better describes it,' he smiled, 'for suddenly I was seeing, and accepting, that the thing I'd never supposed would happen to me had happened! Here was I, yet again going over what you'd said to me, and again reliving how you'd said "I wouldn't marry you"— marriage to anyone never having figured in my plans— when suddenly I just knew that I was in love with you, and not only that but, by thunder, I did want to marry— I wanted to marry you, and only you.'

A long sigh left Farran. Stallard not only loved her, but he wanted to marry her! 'W-was that why you rang me yesterday afternoon?' she asked shyly.

'I'd barely got it sorted out in my head,' he confessed, 'when, still shaken but feeling in urgent need of some contact with you, I found I'd picked up the phone and dialled your number.'

'You said that I'd got something of yours,' Farran remembered huskily.

'I know.' He smiled gently. 'But I was still in shock and my words came out sharp and not as I meant them. But had you asked what that something was, I'd have told you that you had my heart.'

'Oh, no!' Farran cried, aghast at her unfeelingness to him. 'And I, thinking you were referring to the car, asked you to tell me where you wanted it delivered.'

'You weren't to know,' he soothed. 'But it served me right anyway for being so crass as to unthinkingly imagine I could win you as easily as that. When I'd got myself more together, of course, I sat down and did some hard thinking.'

'What, may I ask,' she smiled, 'did your hard thinking bring you?'

'A few basic, if unpalatable, facts,' he replied. 'One being that I'd done nothing to deserve your love and that you'd probably tell me to burn in hell and slam the door on me if I called at your home to see you.'

'Ah—so you decided to enlist Nona's help?'

'She's not an ex-actress for nothing,' he replied. 'Added to which, she's had first-hand experience of your soft heart—she played on that for all she was worth.'

'Honestly!' Farran exclaimed, but not for a moment was she annoyed or angry at being so taken in. She was, in fact, never more grateful to Nona for her assistance. 'Remind me to thank her when I see her,' she beamed.

'Her thanks will be in seeing us happy together,' Stallard told her, and revealed, 'I sometimes think she looks on me as the son she never had.'

Farran underwent a moment of deep sensitivity for him, and then, because she truly felt that they could share everything now, 'Your mother left you when you were small, you...'

'That's right,' Stallard came in with a gentle smile, and seemed in a mind that she must share everything with him when, holding nothing back, he told her, 'She left before I was six months old, but I grew up knowing that she'd married my father for his money, and that he'd had a particularly raw deal where she was concerned.'

'He married late in life, you once told me,' Farran recalled huskily.

'He was nudging fifty,' Stallard confirmed, and went on to confide quietly, 'I thought a lot of him, and it was always a source of regret to me that when he'd spent his prime years working all hours to make his fortune, the only joy he got out of it was to marry a woman who was only after his wealth.'

'He had you for a son,' Farran reminded him, and was hugged warmly for her biased comment.

Then Stallard was telling her, 'A year ago, to my great pleasure, I learned he'd had Nona for a friend.'

'She—er—mentioned one day that she was very close friends with your father,' Farran murmured.

'They were more than close,' he told her. 'Prior to his marriage, Nona was his mistress, and had been for years.'

'But you knew none of this until a year ago?'

'Not a word of it. It was a source of regret to me, as I said, that all my father had known in his life was the toil of hard work, and a woman who, as soon as I arrived to bump up her divorce settlement, was off. Then out of the blue a year ago I received a distressed letter from Nona who, claiming to be an old friend of my father's, said she had no one to turn to for advice on her financial affairs now that he had gone.'

'Naturally you went to see her,' Farran inserted, and received a warm smile for that 'naturally'.

'I did,' he replied, 'and was never more glad of anything than I was of my decision to go and see her that day.'

'You realised, then, that your father had known some happiness in his life.'

'Not at first,' Stallard replied. 'At first, as I looked into her finances, I'd no inkling of how close they'd been. But when I had to tell her that shares which she should have sold but had hung on to were virtually worthless, and she replied with quiet dignity, "I couldn't sell them, Murdoch gave them to me," I knew from the initial amount involved that it must have been quite some friendship.'

'Nona confirmed it?' Farran questioned.

'Reluctantly at first. But a couple of hours later I'd seen pictures of the two of them laughing together, and had been allowed the privilege of reading several of his letters to her which showed, unmistakably, that he'd thought a very good deal of her. At the end of those two hours, to my immense gladness, I knew that prior to their having had an almighty row and going their separate ways my father had had twenty years of happiness in knowing Nona.'

'I'm glad too,' Farran told him warmly, and, gently reaching up to kiss him, asked, 'Did they never think of marrying each other in those twenty years?'

'At the start, they were both too ambitious to want to be tied down. Then, when my father had made it and Nona hadn't, she wouldn't marry him. Oddly, though, shortly after they split up, they both married other people.'

'Nona married someone?'

'Her marriage didn't work either,' Stallard told her. 'Some years later my father and Nona met again, and remained friends until he died. The most heartening thing of all to me, though,' he concluded, 'is that Nona showed me the last letter my father ever wrote to her. It was dated after they met again, and in that letter he wrote, "If you're ever in trouble of any sort and I'm not around—contact my son."'

'Oh, darling!' Farran cried, and knew Stallard had felt as much rewarded to have read that as to know that his father had known quite some happiness in his lifetime. 'So after that you visited her as often as you could?'

'That's right,' he agreed, 'and frequently ferried her to visit her ailing bridge partner.'

'Which is how you came to know Aunt Hetty,' Farran said quietly.

'And, ultimately, became acquainted with my future wife,' Stallard said firmly. Then quickly, and amazing Farran that he still seemed to think there was some doubt about it, 'You are going to marry me, aren't you?' he asked urgently.

'Of course,' she did not delay to tell him, and as a smile that was wonderful to see broke across his features, 'That's how I realised I was in love with you,' she told him lovingly.

'It is?' he questioned, and Farran laughed at his puzzled expression.

'You'd said something about the lucky man I married, the first time you kissed me,' she tried to explain more clearly. 'Anyway,' she rushed on when from the sudden tender expression on his face she knew he was remembering that conversation, 'it was two days later, when I was wondering why the dickens I couldn't get you out of my head, that I suddenly knew that when it came to the man I wanted to marry, I wanted it to be you, because—I was in love with you.'

For some seconds Stallard just sat and looked into her gentle brown eyes, then, 'You beautiful, beautiful, enchanting darling!' he breathed. Then once more he drew her tenderly close to his heart.

Six exciting series for you every month... from Harlequin

HARLEQUIN

Romance®

The series that started it all

Tender, captivating and heartwarming...
love stories that sweep you off to faraway places
and delight you with the magic of love.

◆

Harlequin Presents®

Powerful contemporary love stories...as individual as the women who read them

The No. 1 romance series...
exciting love stories for you, the woman of today...
a rare blend of passion and dramatic realism.

◆

Harlequin Superromance®

It's more than romance... it's Harlequin Superromance

A sophisticated, contemporary romance-fiction
series, providing you with a longer,
more involving read...a richer mix of complex plots,
realism and adventure.

HARLEQUIN
American Romance®
Harlequin celebrates the American woman...

...by offering you romance stories written about American women, by American women for American women. This series offers you contemporary romances uniquely North American in flavor and appeal.

◆

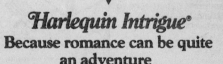

Passionate stories for today's woman

An exciting series of sensual, mature stories of love...dilemmas, choices, resolutions... all contemporary issues dealt with in a true-to-life fashion by some of your favorite authors.

◆

Harlequin Intrigue®
Because romance can be quite an adventure

Harlequin Intrigue, an innovative series that blends the romance you expect... with the unexpected. Each story has an added element of intrigue that provides a new twist to the Harlequin tradition of romance excellence.

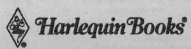